Return of the Flutterbee

James A. Whitney

For Ainslee, Amy, Ann, Britton, Diana, Dina, Grace, Jamison, Jeffrey and Rachel

Prologue

Five Months Ago

The dragon lay bleeding on the snow of the valley floor. It was dead, killed by the force of one too many fireballs. It was a mess of yellowed scales, deep red blood, black soot and white snow.

"We won," said Sylvia Sabane.

Sylvia Sabane appeared to be a young woman, perhaps seventeen years of age. She had straight hair, the pale blonde of fresh cream. She was perhaps five and a half feet tall, though she looked a little bit taller from the slightness of her build. She was dressed in the simple clothes one might find on a farmer's daughter, or perhaps a merchant's daughter.

She did not look like she belonged in a cold valley in late autumn, standing at the corpse of a white dragon.

"That we did," called Jana Aliston from the dragon.

Jana Aliston yanked at the belly of a dragon, pulling loose a scale about two feet in diameter. The scale came loose reluctantly, and Jana lost her balance once it did pull out. She stepped back quickly and regained her composure.

Jana appeared to be ten years Sylvia's senior. She was almost half a foot taller, and her frame was much sturdier. Her hair was the orangish red of the embers of a dying campfire. She had on a leather vest that was at least two sizes too small for her, a dirty white undershirt tied in a knot at her stomach, and a plain skirt. Both the vest and the skirt were covered with glittering gems.

"What are you doing?" asked Sylvia.

"Taking a scale," said Jana. "As proof."

"Proof?" said Sylvia.

"It will be useful to prove to others that we did this," said Jana.

Sylvia shrugged. "That doesn't matter to me," she said. "The dragons will know soon enough. We should prepare for the next one."

Jana shook her head. "I'm not sure there will be a next one."

"It's my destiny," said Sylvia. "And you will help me."

"Yeah," said Jana, "well, let's just get back to Westvalia and see what happens."

"No," said Sylvia. She pointed a finger at Jana and walked over toward her.

Jana stopped moving unnaturally. She appeared frozen in place as Sylvia walked over toward her. Sylvia reached out her hand and placed it on Jana's cheek.

"You see, Jana," said Sylvia, "this is my destiny. Thousands of lost souls cry forth, and have given me power. You know now as well as I do what those souls seek. They seek vengeance. They seek vengeance against the dragons who sent them to their unnatural grave."

Jana blinked, as if it were all she could do. In truth, it was all she could do. Sylvia Sabane was not a simple young girl. Nor was she seventeen. She had been called many names before, first Sylvia Ingham, then the Scourge of Wickerton, then the Globe Theater Villain and finally Sycosina Soulbane. She had taken up hiding in Westvalia, biding her time until her powers found reason, as the simple young girl Sylvia Sabane. Just a month ago, she discovered the reason for her powers.

"I have long said that you would one day become my apprentice," said Sylvia. "Perhaps that is still true, perhaps it is not. But whether I orchestrated it or not, you did slay this dragon. Won't you slay other dragons for me?"

Sylvia circled around Jana and laid her arms on Jana's shoulders. She leaned her cheek against Jana's back. Jana didn't move, or say anything.

"Stop that," said Jamie Wheaton from a distance.

Jamie was a young girl, twelve and a half years of age. She stood a few inches over five feet tall, with a normal frame that was showing its first signs of womanhood. She was dressed simply, much like Sylvia, though she wore a necklace that had three amber gems on it.

"Oh, all right," said Sylvia. She snapped her fingers and Jana lurched forward, freed from the grasp of her spell.

"You know I hate it when you do that," said Jana.

"Yes," said Sylvia, "but at times I like to remind you that I still can."

Jana shook her head. "Friends don't do that to each other."

"Ah," said Sylvia, "but you are still my friend, even as I have. Contradiction? Conundrum? Deny it if you must, but I think you enjoy it."

Jana laughed derisively. Jamie threw up her arms and turned away.

"I think deep down," said Sylvia, "you envy my powers. You now know I have a cause and deep down you wish to be a part of it. Deep down you know you will join me."

"Think whatever you want," said Jana with a dismissive wave of her hand. "I killed this dragon for my own reasons. You helped kill it for your own reasons. We are friends, but I'm not your apprentice."

"Yet," said Sylvia. "Remember that you once begged me to make you my apprentice."

"That was a long time ago," said Jana, "and I'm a very different person now."

"Yes," said Sylvia. "In some ways you are. In some ways you aren't. You never were able to see your own vulnerabilities, your own desires to let the responsibilities fall on someone else's hand."

"Don't be silly," said Jana.

"You killed this dragon because Tybilt wanted you to," said Sylvia.

"I did not," said Jana.

"Are you denying that Tybilt wanted you to kill this dragon?" said Sylvia.

"No," said Jana. "But that's not why I killed her."

"Of course," said Sylvia. "You can't see that now, but you know with absolute certainty that you could blame this plot on him. This is his battle, not your own."

"Don't be silly," said Jana. "The dragon was meddling with the kingdom, pitting mages as the enemies of everyone else. I had every reason to want to kill her for myself."

"But you didn't," said Sylvia. "You didn't, my dear."

Sylvia walked up to Jana and placed her arms on her shoulders. She smiled slightly, looking Jana directly in the eye. Jana shook her head and looked off into the distance.

"You act," said Sylvia, "on the whim of others, convincing yourself only that you are acting on your own regard after the wheels are in motion. When you are successful, as you are now, you can take the credit and the glory for the deeds. But you always prepare yourself for failure by being able to blame someone else for your actions. Had you failed to kill this dragon, you would have consoled yourself into thinking it was all Tybilt's idea anyway."

"That is where we differ, my friend," said Sylvia. "Nobody told me to kill dragons. I do that for my own reasons. My failure to kill this dragon by myself is my own, tempered by your own success. You killed this dragon, not me."

"I killed her because I wanted to," said Jana.

"And I'm grateful," said Sylvia. "Next time, you tell yourself you killed the next dragon because you wanted to. But instead of Tybilt, it will be me that prompted you."

Sylvia stepped back from Jana and laughed softly. Jana shook her head.

"You know I hate it when you do that," she said again.

"I know," said Sylvia. "That's part of the reason I enjoy doing it."

Jana ignored her comment. "We've got to get back to Westvalia," she said. "There are other dragons. This won't go unnoticed. There will be a war."

"Of course," said Sylvia. "A war in which we will kill more dragons."

"We'll see about that," said Jana.

Sylvia smiled and walked away. Jana looked back at the dragon and then to the scale she held in her hand. She shook her head slowly and followed Sylvia back to civilization.

Chapter One

The Next Assignment

"Well done," said Jana.

It had been five months since Jana and Jamie had returned from the frigid northlands. During that five months, Jana continued Jamie's magical training. Jamie had just successfully empowered her fourth gem against eleven earlier failures. This one was different from the previous three—it was a blue topaz rather than orange. According to Jana, that meant it could be more powerful. Jamie came to believe that, as it took her nearly three times as long to empower as the orange gems.

"That took a long time," said Jamie. "I wasn't sure I could do it."

"But you did," said Jana. "As you practice you'll be able to empower them more quickly, but when you get to a ruby or sapphire you will find it takes five times as long."

Jamie nodded.

"That's for another time," said Jana. "For now, take a bit of a rest. You deserve it."

Jamie smiled. She walked to the front room of the house and sat down in her reading chair. She closed her eyes and leaned her head back against the chair. A moment later, her attempt at a nap was interrupted by a loud knock at the door.

"Get that, will you?" yelled Jana. "I'm still cleaning up in here."

Jamie stood up slowly. She ambled over to the door. She opened the door. A moment later, the doorway was filled by a Westvalian Royal Guard.

"Miss Wheaton," the guard said in a voice as deep as the sea.

Jamie looked up. The guard was a full foot and a half taller than she was. With his armor, he was over three times her size. He wore a broad deep blue sash over his left shoulder. Imprinted in a deeper blue was the familiar star and valley representing the Westvalian crown. Underneath the sash was a set of full plate armor. If the armor had seen any battle, its polished sign did not betray it. Above the armor and resting near the arch of the doorway was the stern bald head of the guard. He neither smiled nor frowned as he gazed unblinkingly down at Jamie.

"What do you want?" asked Jamie, hoping to convey the sort of annoyance one might feel toward a trespassing insect.

"I bear a summons for your mentor," said the guard impassively. "Fetch her," he added, as if instructing a dog.

"She's busy," said Jamie. "Come back later."

The guard paused for a moment. "I am afraid that is impossible," the guard said. "Fetch her, child."

"What is this about?" asked Jamie. She was determined not to let her fear of the guard show. Instead, as Jana had instructed her, she would channel that fear into a sense of annoyance.

"King Tybilt requests her presence in the palace gardens," said the guard.

"Requests?" said Jamie. "Very well, I'll let her know and you can be on your way."

"That is impossible, child," said the guard. "My orders are specific. I am to escort her to the palace gardens."

"Then it's not a request, is it?" said Jamie with a sneer.

"If you prefer," said the guard.

"If she can't refuse," said Jamie, "it's a command, not a request."

"I have no desire to continue these semantic games," said the guard. "Out of my way, child."

The guard reached out with his right hand to grasp Jamie's left shoulder. Jamie closed her eyes and stood firm.

"Touch my apprentice, and we'll see what the melting point of that armor really is."

Jamie opened her eyes and grinned, sensing Jana's presence behind her.

"Miss Aliston," said the guard. "King Tybilt requests your presence in the palace gardens."

"For what?" said Jana.

"I was instructed not to say," said the guard.

"You were also ordered to return with me to the palace gardens," said Jana matter-of-factly.

"That is correct," said the guard.

"Which order would you like to disobey?" said Jana.

"I take your point," said the guard.

Jana grinned at the guard. The guard coughed and looked at Jana's feet. A second later, he muttered something below his breath.

"There is an ancient dragon in the palace gardens."

"Really?" blurted out Jamie.

"I am told that it has asked for you by name."

"We'd better go then," said Jana.

It certainly seemed that way to Jamie.

Jana, Jamie and the guard made their way quickly toward the royal palace. A few moments later, they had traversed the hallways of the palace to come to a viewing room at the rear of the palace. King Tybilt and three older men, who Jamie assumed were advisors of some sort, were standing at the back wall looking out the windows.

Without a word of greeting, Jana moved to the back windows and looked out over the gardens. It was a vision that she had seen several times before, and one she quite liked, especially in the beginning of spring. The small trees lining the garden paths were hinting at the bloom they would show in a month. The perennial flowers were beginning to poke their way through the ground. The garden was a green of possibilities.

Today, in the central path leading away from the palace, the garden also contained a large green ancient dragon.

The dragon resembled Norzakind in shape: it was just over fifty feet from head to toe, and the top of his head was a full thirteen feet above the ground. Its body was covered with dark green scales, and its wings were folded in to its sides. Foot long teeth extended down from the top of its mouth over its lower jaw. Atop its head was a tuft of greyish white hair and several horns.

The dragon was scanning the area with its yellow eyes, until its eyes met Jana from behind the window pane. A puff of grey smoke flared from its nostrils. It continued to stare.

"It's Kaseraak!" yelled Jamie after looking upon the dragon for several seconds.

"Kase-who?" remarked one of the advisors.

"How long has he been here?" asked Jana in a soft even-tempered alto.

"One and a half hours," remarked Tybilt.

"Has he done anything?" asked Jana.

"He has only asked for you," said Tybilt. "There was a minor confrontation with the guards when he landed, but he has not attacked them."

"So the guards didn't attack him?" asked Jamie.

"My guards are not suicidal," said Tybilt, "nor would I order them to be."

"I suppose I better go see what he wants," said Jana.

Jana opened the door to the back terrace of the palace. She motioned for Jamie to follow her. The two climbed down the stairs from the terrace to the grounds of the garden. Behind her, Tybilt stepped outside, though he remained on the terrace.

"Jana Aliston," the dragon said as Jana approached her.

"Kaseraak," said Jana without emotion. "What brings you here?"

"This is an ill time," said the dragon. "You have killed my sister."

"She had been provoking a conflict between mages and the kingdom of Westvalia," said Jana, "one that has led to the deaths of many of my friends, including my mentor. She also killed thousands of Westvalian soldiers."

"I am aware of these facts," said Kaseraak. "Whatever her misdeeds were, they do not change what you are. You have slain an ancient dragon."

"I have," said Jana.

"There are now only nine of us left," said Kaseraak. "The desire for retribution stews within the hearts of the other eight."

"But not you?"

"They do not know you as I do," said Kaseraak. "Flawed as you are, you will attempt to do what is just."

"What do you want?" asked Jana.

"Understand, Jana Aliston," Kaseraak said, "we are at the precipice of war. Several dragons believe that the humans are on the verge of releasing the scourge of taconite upon the land yet again. You do know about that, don't you?"

"Norzakind told me about the taconite problem, yes," said Jana. "She also wiped out the human settlement at Jimburgh, which was the only place within a hundred miles of the taconite ore."

"And how long, do you suppose, will it be until your king resettles the northern valley?" asked Kaseraak. "Within the decade, I would imagine."

"A decade is a long time," said Jana.

"Not to an ancient dragon," said Kaseraak.

"True," said Jana.

"I am hoping that, contrary to the feelings of some of my brothers and sisters, that you do not want a war," said Kaseraak. "I assure you, you would find it more difficult to kill nine ancient dragons than one."

"I have no desire to fight another ancient dragon," said Jana.

"Good," said Kaseraak. "But a pledge is not enough to satisfy my brothers and sisters. They demand action to demonstrate your good faith."

"What do you want?" said Jana.

"How much did Norzakind tell you about the Vaspen and their use of taconite?" asked Kaseraak.

"Enough," said Jana. "She said that taconite led to the extinction of many magical creatures."

"Indeed," said Kaseraak. "In particular, there was one magical creature called the flutterbee. It is a large insect, about the size of a young child's fist, with distinctive orange and black stripes. It is mostly harmless. While it has a stinger to protect itself, using it causes its own death, so it will only sting in the defense of its hive."

"Long ago," continued Kaseraak, "the flutterbees were spread throughout the plains of what you call Westvalia. There were perhaps millions of them through the plains, blanketing the land with the soft buzzing sound of their wings."

"What about them?" asked Jana.

"The flutterbee was vital to all magical creatures," said Kaseraak. "Much as with the pollen of the flowers they drank from, the flutterbees spread magical essence through the plains, giving other magical creatures the vital energy they need to reproduce. Without the flutterbees, all magical creatures are destined to go extinct."

"Even you?" said Jamie.

"Yes," said Kaseraak. "Norzakind was the only ancient dragon born within the last two thousand years to survive past the age of eighty."

"A sad tale," said Jana, "but I don't see what I can do about it."

"There remains one hope for ancient dragons," said Kaseraak. "Seventy miles south of Cape Charles there is a group of islands called the Cuttyhunk Isles."

"That's just a myth," said Jana. "Nobody's ever seen them."

"They exist," said Kaseraak, "but they are protected by magic, a form of magic that hides them from the rest of the world."

"Like Anna's house!" said Jamie.

"Every four hundred twenty-seven years," said Kaseraak, "for two weeks tides are low enough to allow three reefs to surface between Cape Charles and the Cuttyhunk Isles. During this time, we ancient dragons can use those reefs as resting points to travel between the mainland and the isles. That is how we know of those islands, and how we can monitor those islands."

"Let me guess," said Jana. "It has been four hundred twenty six years and eleven months since the last low tide."

"No," said Kaseraak. "It has been two hundred ninety-eight years."

"So what, then?" asked Jana.

"The island was untouched by the Vaspen or by taconite," said Kaseraak. "There are several flutterbee hives spread throughout the island."

"You want me to bring one back," said Jana.

"Precisely," said Kaseraak.

"What's in it for me?" asked Jana.

"You mean apart from preventing a war between humans and ancient dragons?" asked Kaseraak. "I would have thought better of you than that."

"Yes," said Jana, "apart from that."

"Consider then," said Kaseraak. "You are a mage. Your livelihood depends upon the magic ancient dragons emit. Without us, you are powerless. But if you bring back a flutterbee hive, and the flutterbees flourish again, you will have an abundant supply of magic. You would be the savior of magic."

"Hm," said Jana. "I'll think about it."

"I suggest you do so quickly," said Kaseraak. "My brothers are normally quite patient, but they are not where the death of their sister is concerned."

"I understand," said Jana.

With that, Kaseraak spread his wings open, spreading thirty-six feet to either side of his body. With several flaps, he rose to the sky, as effortlessly as a small bird might. A minute later, he was a mere speck in the distant sky.

"Come on," said Jana. "I bet Tybilt has a few things to say to us now."

"No," said Tybilt.

"No what?" asked Jana.

"I am aware of the conversation you had with that dragon," said Tybilt. "You wish to ask me a question, and the answer to that question is 'no'."

"What question did you think I was going to ask?"

"You were about to ask whether I had an opinion for you on whether to voyage to the Cuttyhunk Isles for that dragon."

"And you don't?"

"No," said Tybilt. "Not for you," he added after a few seconds.

"Then for whom?" asked Jana. "My apprentice?"

"Does it matter?" said Tybilt. "Whatever I say to you, you will do the exact opposite anyway. You're contrary that way."

"Perhaps you should tell me the opposite of what you want then," said Jana. "Throw me off."

"You already know what I'm going to say anyway," said Tybilt.

"That I'm a fool for even considering helping an ancient dragon?" asked Jana. "That I should let them die?"

Tybilt thought for a moment. "Close," he said.

"Close?" said Jana.

"I wouldn't call you a fool," said Tybilt.

"But you would think it," said Jana.

"No," said Tybilt, "I wouldn't. I can understand why you might want to help the dragons."

"You can?" said Jana.

"They're the only reason you can practice magic," said Tybilt. "That much I've learned."

Jana nodded.

"Unfortunately for you," said Tybilt, "I have to put that aside in the name of the greater good of the kingdom. Magic has been a disruptive force in our land for decades, if not centuries. It has been held by a privileged few, some of whom thought to use such power to usurp the right of the throne. Like your mentor."

"I'm not Vissara," said Jana.

"For many years you were," said Tybilt.

"But now you need me," said Jana. "If there is to be a war against the ancient dragons, magic is your only hope. You must recognize that."

"I don't think there will be a war," said Tybilt. "If it's war they wanted, they would have attacked by now. Something's holding them back. I fear that it's your presence."

"There's not much I could do if nine ancient dragons decided to attack Westvalia," said Jana. "I can't be nine places at once."

"But you could be in one place," said Tybilt. "That would be a start."

"I don't see where that gets us," said Jana.

"I'd invite you to consider the possibility that the ancient dragons would rather attack Westvalia with you gone, off on a hopeless adventure in the South Seas."

"That's a possibility," said Jana.

"It's a risk I can't afford to take," said Tybilt.

"It's not your decision," said Jana.

"No," said Tybilt, "it isn't."

"So you did have an opinion for me," said Jana.

"You know I did," said Tybilt.

"I think you're worried about what would happen if I succeeded," said Jana.

"Succeeded?" said Tybilt. "All right, this I want to hear. Why am I afraid of your success?"

"Magic would be back," said Jana, "back in a way far stronger than you've ever experienced before. It's a force that the throne can't control. You're afraid of losing your kingdom."

Tybilt laughed. "I am?"

"You are," said Jana. "If I succeed, magic will be such a powerful force that even a common peasant could learn to control it. It will be able to create mountains out of sheer will, just as the Noonmark Spire was created to be due south of Hockessin. Just as the marshes underneath Theoton were raised to form solid ground for that city. Did you think those were natural things? No, magic did that."

Tybilt laughed again. "You have a wonderful imagination," said Tybilt.

"You deny that a mage could do such things?" said Jana.

"It doesn't matter to me," said Tybilt. "Contrary to what you're thinking, I have read books on magic. I know how it works. I also know that even if you succeed it will take decades if not centuries for your success to have an effect. I will be long gone before the flutterbee spreads across the southwestern plains, assuming that one hive will be sufficient to allow that. It will take a millenia for the ancient dragons to repopulate. But there is something else."

"Oh?" asked Jana.

"Yes," said Tybilt. "Something a beautiful young girl once told me."

"What's that?" asked Jana.

"She told me that the throne has nothing to fear from mages as long as its rule is just," said Tybilt.

Jana blushed. Jamie blinked at Jana. It was the first time in a while Jana had been at a loss for words.

"I have always believed your words, Jana," said Tybilt. "That is why, in time, I sought to reconcile with you. That was why I sought to cooperate with your apprentice. You know now that I believe magic is essential for the defense of our kingdom. But there is more."

"I have always tried to rule justly," said Tybilt. "A great leader, however, must think not only of himself but of the future of his kingdom. How can I influence the behavior of future kings? I recognize from my own failings the danger of thinking one had power above all; it led me to continue a senseless war that almost destroyed our greatest defense against the ancient dragons who think themselves the rulers of this land. How can I ensure that future kings will rule justly?"

"Powerful mages?" asked Jana.

"Precisely," said Tybilt. "That and a kingdom running efficiently and fairly so that the grand majority of mages are willing to back the throne. I believe that, were it not for the personal animosity between my father and your mentor, we could have had that. I believe that with our reconciliation we can achieve that. I know there are other mages remaining, those who hid from our forces rather than confront us directly. Over time, they will once again trust the kingdom enough to serve it. I may not live to see that day, but I can work toward it."

"So you want me to succeed?" said Jana in disbelief.

"It is for the long term good of the kingdom," Tybilt said. He sighed and turned around, looking off at a distant wall.

"But?" Jana asked, sensing some reservation.

"There are appearances to consider," said Tybilt.

"Appearances!" said Jana. "Who cares about that aristocratic nonsense?"

"It is not the aristocracy about which I am worried," said Tybilt.

"Then who?" said Jana.

"The dragons," said Tybilt.

"What about them?" said Jana.

"For many years, probably more than I can count, the dragons have meddled in human affairs," said Tybilt. "They have treated us like playthings. Now comes a time when they depend on us for help. I do not think we should be so eager to give it."

"So you would refrain from doing something that's in our best interests out of spite?" asked Jana.

"You of all people should be familiar with that sentiment," said Tybilt.

"What?" said Jana angrily.

"Never mind," said Tybilt, seeming to back away from the accusation. "No, it is not out of spite. I am thinking of our relations with the dragons. I am hoping to move beyond being their playthings. I am hoping that they will come to respect our existence."

"How do you do that?" said Jana.

"Consider, for a moment, how it would appear to a dragon if I lent you my full support," said Tybilt. "I could, for instance, send a fleet of ships at your command to seek out the Cuttyhunk Isles, a thousand of my finest sailors to help you face whatever perils await you. What would that say to the dragons?"

"That you're willing to help them?" said Jana.

"Not only willing," said Tybilt, "but eager. I'd go as far to say zealous. It would give them the impression that the kingdom responds to their orders. Why would we do that? Out of fear of what they might do if we refuse to comply."

"You don't fear them?" said Jana.

"Of course I do," said Tybilt. "One dragon alone apparently wiped out my entire force at Jimburgh. I think it would take my entire army to fend off an attack of perhaps three of them. But nine, working in concert? For that I would need magic, and a fair bit of luck. You and I both know that."

Jana nodded.

"But they don't know that," said Tybilt. "For all they know, we have a hundred mages waiting to defend the city. Or perhaps we have a cunning plan of defense. I can't let them see that we don't."

"So what do you want me to do?" said Jana.

"What do you think you should do?" asked Tybilt.

"I don't know," said Jana. "Kaseraak wants me to voyage to an island no one has ever heard of, capture a hive of flutterbees, whatever they are, and then return to the plains so that the flutterbees can repopulate the area. Doing so would apparently save the ancient dragons from a certain extinction. There's something about it that doesn't sit right with me."

"What's that?" asked Tybilt.

"Why me?" said Jana. "Why now? Presumably this is not a new problem of theirs. The flutterbee didn't just disappear yesterday. They've had hundreds, if not thousands of years to go about doing this. So why didn't the dragons get someone else to do it? Why didn't Kaseraak ask Lady Vissara long ago? They seemed to get along well. For that matter, why haven't they already done this themselves? Why involve humans at all?"

"Maybe they can't carry the hive?" suggested Jamie.

"The dragons are capable of summoning human avatars," said Jana, "some of which have infiltrated the kingdom and furthered their interests. I don't think it's for a lack of hands that they haven't done it yet."

"No," said Tybilt, "that does sound curious."

Jana and Tybilt stood in silence for half a minute while they pondered the problem. Jamie glanced between both of them. She couldn't figure anything out, either.

"I wish," said Jana, "sometimes I wish you would just order me to do something, so that I could confidently do the opposite."

Tybilt laughed. "All right then," said Tybilt, "I order you to charge blindly off on this mission, without second thought."

Jana laughed.

"In truth," said Tybilt, "the decision is yours. I can only hope to impress on you the interests of the kingdom. Further, for the sake of appearances, should you decide to take the dragon's mission, the kingdom cannot assist you. I won't prevent you from doing anything, and personally I would wish you success, but you would have to do it on your own."

Jana nodded. "I understand."

"I think we should do it," said Jamie.

"Oh?" asked Jana.

"There's something that seems right about it," said Jamie. "The flutterbees sound neat. Plus it would be an adventure! I like adventure."

"If only it were that simple," said Jana.

"It can be," said Jamie.

"No, it can't," said Jana. "Nothing ever is."

The three stood silently for several seconds.

"Usually I have a gut feeling about things like this," said Jana. "Usually I would jump at the idea, especially if I thought you might disapprove. That's what I thought you were going to say, that you didn't want me gone, and that you needed me to defend Westvalia from a potential attack."

"I do need you for that," said Tybilt.

"No, you don't," said Jana. "There are others who will help against the dragons. There is at least one person that I know of who would be more than eager to battle the dragons again. You know of her."

"I shudder to think," said Tybilt, "that the defense of Westvalia might depend on the villain of the Globe Theater Massacre."

"She would fight by your side," said Jana. "In fact, I worry about what she might think of the flutterbee rescue adventure. I can't imagine she'd approve of anything that would prolong the lives of the ancient dragons."

"Still," said Tybilt, "I hope it doesn't come to that."

"I think going to get the flutterbee is worth it, if it averts a war between the dragons and the kingdom. But there's something I don't know. There's something Kaseraak didn't tell me about the island, or why they haven't done this already. I need to know that before I can make my mind up."

Tybilt nodded.

"It is, as you've said many times, a trust issue," said Jana. "They've been playing mages against the rest of humanity for some time, perhaps out of fear, or perhaps just to amuse themselves. I'm inclined to help them, but only if they respect me. I need to find that out. The only way for me to do that is to go talk to Kaseraak directly."

"I suppose you'd better do that, then," said Tybilt.

"I suppose I should," said Jana.

Chapter Two

Briefing

"How do we know he'll even be there?" asked Jamie.

She posed the question to Jana while the pair rode northeast to the mountain town of Bracken. The pair had joined up with a larger caravan. It was quite common for people to venture from Westvalia to Bracken in the spring, now that the weather was warm enough to permit Bracken's primary industry, lumber farming, to commence. They rode alongside all sorts of people hoping for work in the foothills of the Ursidae Mountains.

"We don't," said Jana.

Jamie and Jana were not travelling to Bracken to cut down trees. Their destination lay two further days into the mountains: a dark cave on the side of a large mountain. Their destination was the home of Kaseraak, one of the nine surviving ancient dragons, and the only one who Jamie and Jana knew by name.

"What if he isn't?" asked Jamie.

Jana sighed. She couldn't fault Jamie for trying to make conversation. It was a long ride, and they had to talk about something.

"He will be," said Jana. "He has to be expecting me."

"But you just said…" said Jamie, her voice trailing off.

"I don't," said Jana. "I don't know. I don't know what to expect from him anymore. I just hope he remembers that he owes us his life."

Jamie shuddered. She remembered the time they first met Kaseraak, long ago. Jana's former apprentice Isabella, then working for Tybilt, had set off to slay the ancient dragon. Jana and Jamie attacked her from behind, throwing off her careful orchestration of the fight against Kaseraak. Without Jana's interference, Kaseraak would have likely died.

Since that time, Jamie had come to think of Kaseraak as her dragon friend. Jana had sought him out for advice, much as her mentor had sought him out for advice earlier. His counsel seemed to be sound; he wouldn't always have the right solution, but he would be able to guide Jana to a decision that worked out well.

The situation changed dramatically the previous fall. Jana discovered that an ancient dragon named Norzakind had been meddling in human affairs. At the time, the dragon had been disrupting mining operations in the northern village of Jimburgh. But that was not the full extent of her interference. Jana discovered that three decades earlier, Norzakind had used an avatar, a human projection under her control, to set off a conflict between mages and the kingdom. It was Norzakind's doing that led to a ban on magic within the kingdom of Westvalia.

Three decades ago, the great archmage Solanche had discovered Norzakind's treachery. Solanche took Norzakind's acts as those led by all ancient dragons, and decided to strike against the one ancient dragon she knew: Kaseraak. Using a pendant that protected her from all forms of physical harm, she battled Kaseraak nearly to submission. Late in the battle, Kaseraak was able to separate Solanche from her pendant, spelling her own doom.

In the ensuing two decades, the relations between mages and the kingdom began to thaw. The ban on mages became one in name only, and several mages earned their way into prominent positions in Westvalia's aristocracy. One of those mages was Lady Elizabeth Vissara, Jana's mentor. Vissara was very closely involved with King Escalis, Tybilt's father.

In truth, as Jana later discovered, Vissara was plotting against the kingdom. She formed the Circle of Eight, which was to be a group of eight mages set to replace the king and rule over the land. On the night of the First Bloom Ball eleven years ago, Vissara announced her intentions to King Escalis. This started a new war against mages, and made the young Jana an enemy of the throne.

Jana would later discover that during the time leading up to that fateful night, Kaseraak had been advising Vissara to revolt against the throne. Vissara wrote in her private journals of her plans, noting several times where Kaseraak had approved or suggested alternatives. In Jana's mind there was no doubt that Kaseraak was doing what Norzakind had done two decades earlier: plant a wedge between mages and the kingdom.

In the decade after the war on mages started, Jana didn't have time to worry about what Kaseraak had told Vissara. She was too worried about her own survival. Eight years ago, Vissara succeeded in her ambition to topple the king of Westvalia; she stabbed him through the heart, killing him. This brought Prince Tybilt to the throne.

Tybilt was at once more vicious and more cunning than his father. A few months after his father's death, Tybilt cornered Vissara and Jana. Vissara was captured, but Jana escaped with her life. Since that time, Jana had been plotting to bring Tybilt's kingdom down, but without the sort of direction that could result in lasting change. Under Tybilt's rule, the entire land came under Westvalia's rule, save for a few barbarian tribes to the far north. Tybilt had won, or so it seemed.

Two years ago, that began to change. Taking Kaseraak's initial advice to heart, Jana led an insurrection against Westvalia in the formerly independent city of Hockessin. Westvalia's forces in the area were weak because Tybilt had ordered the bulk of his army to assist in conquering the northern barbarians. Those forces were weakened again in a foolhardy attack against the infamous and vicious necromancer Sycosina Soulbane. Hockessin's forces, led by Jana, were able to dispatch the remaining Westvalian troops with ease.

The next spring Jana attempted to spread the insurrection west, this time to the mountain town of Bracken. Unlike Hockessin, Tybilt was prepared for this attempt. He had ordered the mayor of Bracken to poison the town's wells if an insurrection grew in strength, counting on the resulting panic and the Westvalian control of the poison's antidote to quell any insurrection. This plan was never needed. Jana, when she discovered the plan, became disheartened, unable to contemplate sacrificing so many people for what seemed to be a personal vendetta against Tybilt. She decided their war must end.

Surprisingly, Tybilt agreed. By this time, Tybilt had discovered Norzakind's interference in the northern hinterlands and realized that a war between humanity and the dragons was brewing. He came to believe that magic was the only means to defeat the dragons. His relentless pursuit of mages had left the kingdom without magical protection; most mages had scattered to far flung towns to hide from the powerful Westvalian army. Moreover, as a result of many years worth of propaganda and battles with Jana, most of the Westvalian citizenry had come to distrust or loathe magic. He needed to do something dramatic to reverse that. He asked her to marry him. His hope was that such a union would ally Jana and other mages with Westvalia in a potential war against the dragons.

Jana was shocked at the question. For the first time in Jamie's experience with Jana, Jana was at a loss for words. She decided she needed to think about the question. For the next month, she traveled far across the land, seeking advice from her father, her sister, and several friends. Ultimately she came to talk to Sycosina Soulbane, the one person Westvalia may have hated more than Jana. The two hatched a plan that would enable both Jana and Sycosina to re-enter Westvalian society without committing herself to an alliance with the throne. The two staged a battle at Jana's wedding, ending with Jana seemingly destroying the feared necromancer and saving the Westvalian royal family from certain death at her hands.

After the battle at her wedding, Jana became a hero to the land. Just as Jana, Sycosina and even Tybilt had hoped, the war against magic had been forgotten, with Jana's prior acts against the kingdom forgiven. A few months later, Tybilt had a mission for Jana—discover the cause of disruption and sabotage at Westvalia's mining operations in the cold northern valley of Jimburgh. Tybilt all but knew that a dragon was behind the sabotage. He did not tell Jana of his suspicions, however, preferring to let Jana discover the extent of the dragons' treachery on her own.

Jana started by reviewing Archmage Solanche's journals, hoping to find evidence of a spell by which a person or thing projected an avatar. In time, she discovered that the white dragon Norzakind was behind the sabotage at Jimburgh. She listened to the dragon's explanation for her actions: Westvalia was close to discovering taconite, a mineral that in the past had proved highly toxic to all magical creatures, including the ancient dragons. Norzakind warned Jana that if humans were to discover taconite, the dragons would be forced to destroy human civilization as they had humanity's predecessors, the Vaspen. Jana relayed this information to Tybilt, suggesting that he withdraw from Jimburgh. Tybilt refused, and sent a battalion full of troops to battle Norzakind. The battalion was wiped out, with only three survivors alive to tell the tale of the slaughter.

Jana felt guilty about being unable to prevent the slaughter. She was compelled to complete her review of Solanche's journals. As she reached the end, she learned of Solanche's discovery that Norzakind had been to blame for the initial ban on magic. She had a sudden realization that the dragons were at fault for the war on mages, driving Westvalia away from magic and dividing the forces that might oppose the ancient dragons. The rage she had once felt for Tybilt had a new target: Norzakind.

Jana and Jamie joined forces with Sycosina to face Norzakind. By this time, Sycosina (who now called herself Sylvia) had discovered that she obtained her powers from the dead spirits of the Vaspen, who desired nothing more than the end to all ancient dragons to avenge the genocide of their race. Jana, Sylvia and Jamie battled Norzakind. Jana won, killing the dragon with vicious blasts of fire.

"Do you believe what Kaseraak said about the other dragons?" Jamie asked after reviewing her memory.

"About wanting to kill all of humanity?" asked Jana.

"Yes," said Jamie.

"I think it's a bluff," said Jana. "Unfortunately, I'm not certain, and I'm not willing to push that just yet."

"No," said Jamie.

"I think if they were serious about destroying Westvalia," Jana said, "they would have taken some sort of action. I can't believe Kaseraak was able to hold off all eight other dragons from attacking. From what we saw of Norzakind, they seem to be a more fractured bunch."

Jamie nodded. She didn't really understand, but she nodded to keep Jana talking.

"I just think there has to be more to this than Kaseraak's letting on," said Jana. "They can't have just figured out they need the flutterbee. The question is, why do they need me?"

Jamie shook her head. She didn't know the answer to that one.

The pair made their way to Kaseraak's cave. They spent a nice night at the Deer Run Camp in Bracken, and set out on foot the next day north from the town. The spring air was still chilly in the foothills north of Bracken, and Jamie had to use her magic to keep her warm. A day and a half later, they were at the mouth of Kaseraak's cave.

"I was wondering when you would show up," said Kaseraak from inside the cave.

"I don't have wings to travel," said Jana.

"Come inside," said Kaseraak.

Kaseraak's voice was normally soothing for Jamie, but there was something in the way he said "come inside" that made Jamie twitch. She reached to tug at Jana's hand but Jana was already moving inside.

"Something isn't right," said Jamie to Jana, but Jana evidently couldn't hear her.

The cave hadn't changed much since Jamie saw it last. It had a round opening that was fairly large as caves go, but Jamie wondered how Kaseraak was able to fit through it. The dragon seemed so large to her, never more so as he loomed in the back of the large cavern.

"Have you come to accept the task I have assigned you?" asked Kaseraak.

"Not yet," said Jana. "I have some questions."

"I see," said Kaseraak. "That's unfortunate."

"Unfortunate?" asked Jana.

Jamie fell to the ground and covered her ears as an overwhelmingly loud high-pitched screech echoed throughout the cavern. She glanced up in pain and saw that Jana had not moved.

"I thought I had made myself clear," said Kaseraak. "You really don't have any choice in the matter."

"There is always a choice," said Jana.

The front of the cavern rumbled. The room darkened as something blocked the entrance to the cavern.

"Jana?" said Jamie. She crawled up to her knees and looked out at the front of the cavern.

"I'd like you to meet someone," said Kaseraak. "Jana Aliston, this is Ceredos."

Jana looked back toward the opening of the cave. Blocking it stood a dragon, its scales black as the darkness of the cave. A plume of white smoke emerged from its nostril. Ceredos did not look happy.

Chapter Three

Or Else

"You see, Jana Aliston," said Ceredos, "you have very little choice about the matter."

"Jana!" said Jamie. Jamie felt panic well inside her. There was no exit for her, apparently no option but to fight her way out.

"There's always a choice," said Jana. She shook her right hand. A second later, her hand was engulfed in flame.

"I don't think you want to do that," said Kaseraak. "There are two of us, and this is a very tight space for two dragons. You wouldn't stand a chance."

"And neither would you," said Jana. "Maybe not now. Maybe you would survive this encounter but then where would you be? You came to me because you needed my help. Without me, ancient dragons are going to suffer a slow death. You know this. I know this. So drop the threats."

"You are a fool, Kaseraak," said Ceredos. "She can't help us. She won't help us. We should avenge our sister and be done with it."

"No, please!" yelled Jamie, her gaze alternating between the dragons rapidly. "We want to help you. We wouldn't be here if we didn't. Please stop, we'll do what you say. Don't kill us, I don't want to die. Please. I love dragons. We never wanted to hurt Norzakind."

"Jamie," Jana said through clenched teeth, "be quiet."

"The young one speaks the truth," said Kaseraak. "If she didn't feel the need to help us, she would not be here. She would be preparing for war. She wants to avert a war as much as I do."

"I don't need to do anything," said Jana.

"See?" said Ceredos. "She will not do as we ask. We should kill her now. She is a risk to us all."

Jana turned to face Ceredos directly. "I'm not afraid of you," she said. "You need me, and you and I both know this. You're not going to kill me. Either drop your threats or I'll show you how Norzakind felt."

"You dare to speak to an ancient dragon this way?" said Ceredos.

The two stared at each other intently. Jamie crouched to the ground, shivering. Jana's hand was still encased in flame. Smoke flared from Ceredos's nostrils. Fifteen seconds later, Kaseraak broke the silence.

"She has called your bluff, Ceredos," said Kaseraak. "Back down and let us discuss her task more rationally. A battle would do none of us any good and we all know that."

Ceredos snorted. "Fine," he said. "I hope you know what you're doing."

The fire in Jana's hand disappeared into smoke. Jana stared intently at Ceredos.

"I am here," Jana said, "because I am willing to help you. But there are two things I need to make clear first."

"What?" said Ceredos with a sigh of impatience. He obviously did not take well to being beaten.

"If I succeed at this task," said Jana, "flutterbees will roam the land, spreading their magic. Mages will have power that they haven't seen in centuries, or even millenia. We'll be able to bend the very earth to our will, creating things like the Noonmark spire or the raised ground under Theoton. I've seen this. I know this. You know it too."

"Perhaps," said Ceredos.

"In the meantime, it will take years before the flutterbees' magic allows you ancient dragons to bear children. And after that, a few centuries before the children are old enough to do much more than squak for food. You will be entering a time when humanity is powerful, and you are not."

"Perhaps," said Kaseraak.

"You have to take that chance," said Jana, "or else ancient dragons will die. You know this. I know this. You'd better get used to the prospect."

"If you have a point," said Ceredos, "make it."

"You will no longer be able to treat humans as you do now," said Jana. "We will no longer be things to observe, here for your amusement. We will be able to control your fate, not the other way around. You may as well get used to it now."

"That is an interesting prediction, Miss Aliston," said Ceredos. "I foresee something completely different, should you succeed. But I feel no need to share with you my own vision of the future. You will discover it soon enough."

"Let us take, for the moment, that we will need to be more respectful of humanity," said Kaseraak. "What bearing does that have on our discussion?"

"You need to treat me as an equal," said Jana. "You are keeping things from me, of this I am sure. I cannot attempt this mission without learning everything you know about it. I need more information."

"All right," said Kaseraak. "What would you like to know?"

"Why now?" said Jana.

"Why not now?" asked Kaseraak.

"Why not fifteen years ago?" said Jana. "Why didn't you ask Vissara to do it? Or, for that matter, one of Solanche's contemporaries? You've known about this problem for some time now. Why me?"

"This is true," said Kaseraak.

"And for that matter," said Jana, "why bother with humans at all? You've had centuries to go get the flutterbees yourselves. I know that you can summon human avatars, who should be able to do whatever humans would need to do. Why not just do it yourself?"

"The explanation is long and complicated," said Kaseraak.

"I've got time," said Jana.

"Very well then," said Kaseraak. "I'll let Ceredos explain."

"Five thousand years ago," Ceredos began, "the dominant hominids in the land were called the Vaspen."

"Hominid?" Jamie whispered to Jana.

"Things that walk on two legs," said Jana. "Don't interrupt."

"The times were very different then," said Ceredos, "as I'm sure you can imagine. Specifically, the flutterbees and other magical creatures were spread throughout the land. Magic was abundant, and the Vaspen knew how to use it. Their society spread throughout the land, primarily in small towns and villages. Their magic could do wonderful things, some of which are still with us today."

"That came to an end when the Vaspen discovered taconite," said Ceredos. "Taconite seemed very useful to them, but it was a slow toxin to all magical creatures. The more the Vaspen used taconite, the sicker the magical creatures like the flutterbee became. In time, we had to act, but I fear we acted too slowly."

"We cleansed the land of taconite," said Ceredos, "in the process destroying all that existed of Vaspen society. But we were too late to save the magical creatures of the plains and woodlands. The flutterbee, the wunderboar, the tapping snurtle, and the pixmees all perished. The only magical creatures that survived were the ursidae in the remote mountains, and a few of us ancient dragons."

"I was there," said Ceredos. "It was a dark time. Most of my brothers and sisters perished in their heroic attempts to rid the land of taconite. We succeeded, but the cost was enormous."

"Yes," said Jana, "I heard all this from Norzakind. What does that have to do with me?"

"What Norzakind didn't tell you," said Ceredos, "quite possibly because she never knew any differently, is that the taconite did grave harm to the eggs of dragons. Before taconite, the shell of a dragon's egg was half an inch thick. After the taconite, and without the magic of the flutterbee, the shell became a tenth as thick. Numerous times we dragons have attempted to lay our eggs, and numerous times they have broken from the most mundane of circumstance. In the last two thousand years, only one egg has successfully hatched. That was Norzakind."

"And you think the flutterbees will fix that?" said Jana.

"It is difficult to explain the workings of our reproductive process to someone who has not experienced it," said Ceredos. "But yes, the flutterbees should help that."

"So what happened with this island?" said Jana. "How do you know that flutterbees are there?"

"A few hundred years ago," said Ceredos, "we discovered the Cuttyhunk Isles quite by accident. They were hidden by a rather intricate and delicate magic that, for those without the ability to see through it, wrapped the seas around the islands. Even if you were traveling directly toward the islands, your course would be diverted ever so subtly that you would just go around them."

"We discovered the islands," said Ceredos, "not by breaking through the magic, but by detecting the magic in the first place. The thinking was that the magic must be concealing something, and that by breaking through the magic we were able to discover the island. That was when we learned something new."

"What was that?" said Jana.

"The islands were moving," said Ceredos. "They were moving south at a rate of slightly less than a half a foot per day. This was barely perceptible in the short run, but over several millenia this had the effect of moving the islands further off shore. When we discovered them, the islands were one hundred thirty miles off shore. They are now about one hundred fifty miles off shore."

"The interesting thing about the islands is what happens if you interpret their movements backwards. If they're moving at a certain rate that seems to be the same, you can figure out when the islands were connected to the mainland."

"When was that?" asked Jamie.

"A little over five thousand years ago," said Ceredos. "Just before the Vaspen discovered taconite."

"What happened?"

"We've been able to piece together very litte," said Ceredos. "But what we think happened was that a group of the Vaspen foresaw the disaster that taconite would bring upon their society. Rather than accept their fate, they determined to isolate themselves from the rest of the land, using magic to separate their island from the mainland. They then used their magic to cloak their existence from the rest of the land."

"So wait a second," said Jana. "You've pieced these things together? You don't know?"

"One of the problems with establishing contact with a group with such separatist ideals is that they tend to be mistrustful of anything and everything. No ancient dragon has been able to safely land on the islands for longer than five minutes before having to retreat from vicious magical attacks. It is quite likely that whatever allowed the inhabitants of the island to foresee the Vaspen's demise also allowed them to foresee that ancient dragons would be the instrument of their ultimate destruction. However, we do know that the powerful magic which moves the islands and which protects them from discovery must have a source. There are likely magical creatures there, including the flutterbee."

"Likely?" said Jana.

"I would bet my life on it," said Ceredos.

"Or you would bet mine," said Jana.

"If you prefer to think of it in that way," said Ceredos.

"So let me get this straight," said Jana. "You think that there's a group of these Vaspen still living on those islands. They are preventing you from staying on the island for more than five minutes. They're likely to be mistrustful of outsiders. And you think, but don't know, that there are flutterbees on that island?"

"Yes," said Ceredos.

"And you expect me to go there and get a hive of flutterbees for you?" said Jana.

"Yes," said Ceredos. "The fate of both of our kinds depends on it."

"Forget it," said Jana. "There's no way. If these Vaspen really exist, they wield magical power on a scale so much higher than mine that anyone who approaches the island would be helpless. They won't let you take away some flutterbees. I can't see any reason why they would let me. I doubt I'd even survive an encounter. If they can separate an island from the mainland, what chance do my fireballs have?"

"You are our best hope," said Ceredos.

"I'm not that much hope!" said Jana. "I can't move islands!"

"No," said Ceredos, "but you have a fair chance of getting to the islands undetected. You aren't a magical creature, so they wouldn't necessarily be watching for or even expecting you. Above that, you can use your own magic to mask your presence, and should the situation call for it, your familiarity with magic should help you in a magic-rich environment. Sending an ordinary human wouldn't work because he wouldn't be able to find the island. Sending an army wouldn't work because it would be too overt. It requires subtlety and daring, two things you have proven yourself capable of. You are the best hope for both our kinds."

"Both our kinds?" said Jana. "I don't see why humans need flutterbees at all."

"I was referring not to humans," said Ceredos, "but to mages. Your kind dies with us."

"I see," said Jana.

"Unfortunately," said Kaseraak, "I can't think of any other way that we can help you. There's a lot we don't know about the islands too. The bit about going there every four hundred and whatever years? I made that up as a joke. We've tried to get there."

"What drives you away?" said Jana.

"Magic," said Kaseraak. "It's hard to describe exactly, but it's not unlike a loud high pitched sound would be to you. We depend on our own magical essence to guide us. Somehow, the Vaspen on that island have learned to turn that against us."

"But not me?" asked Jana.

"I hope not," said Kaseraak.

"I see," said Jana. "Give me some time to confer with my apprentice."

Kaseraak nodded slowly. "Of course."

"Outside," Jana said.

Ceredos moved to the side of the cavern to allow Jana and Jamie to pass. Jana and Jamie walked out to the outside of the cavern. Jana sat down on a rock a few feet away from the ledge and looked to the valley below. Jamie sat down beside her.

"So what do you make of this, sprite?" asked Jana.

"I think we should do it," said Jamie.

"Why?" asked Jana.

"Because," said Jamie. "It's right. It seems right to me. The flutterbees should never have died off. They should be there now. We can put things right."

"It will be very dangerous," said Jana.

"That's never stopped us before," said Jamie.

Jana laughed. "No, I suppose not."

"It's the right thing to do," said Jamie. "Even if it doesn't avert a war I think we should do it."

"Okay, sprite," said Jana. "That's good enough for me."

Jana and Jamie went back inside.

"Okay," said Jana, "we'll do it. But I need one more piece of information."

"What's that?" asked Kaseraak.

"The islands," said Jana. "You said you've been there. Where exactly are they?"

"They are almost two hundred miles due south of what you humans call the Bisconty Bay," said Kaseraak.

"Good enough for me," said Jana.

"Miss Aliston," said Ceredos, "I wish you luck. The fate of both our kinds depends on your success."

"We'll see about that," said Jana.

Chapter Four

Old Friends

Jana and Jamie made their way back to Bracken. Going downhill was a fair bit easier than going up the mountains, and Jana and Jamie made fair time. Once they were back in Bracken, they made their way to the Deer Run Camp and rested for a few days.

During that time, Jana penned a letter to Tybilt. She started the letter and then stopped three separate times as she considered what to say. In the end, she kept it simple:

"Dear Tybilt," wrote Jana, "I am going to the south seas to get a flutterbee hive. See you when I return."

Jana gave the letter to a messenger the next morning. She and Jamie then took the road east toward the coastal city of Hockessin.

"It's time to cash in some favors," said Jana.

"Westley?" asked Jamie.

"Him," said Jana, "and Anna too. Maybe Mallory."

Two years ago, Jana had led a group of rebels against Westvalian forces in Hockessin. Westley and Mallory led the revolution by Jana's side. Anna was Jana's sister, and she helped win the fight for Hockessin as well.

Jana went to see Westley first. After arriving in Hockessin, she went down to the docks, hoping to find him there. She was in luck.

Westley was standing at the end of a dock, watching workers unload some parcels off a small ship.

"Westley Roberts," Jana said as she approached.

"Jana Aliston," Westley said with practiced nonchalance.

Westley Roberts was an experienced sailor, old for the business but not quite ready to get out of it yet. He had a mop of light brown hair on his head and a winning but slightly crooked smile. His muscles were lean from years of physical labor, and his skin was tanned from his time on the open sea. He was ever so slightly shorter than Jana, but he still cut a commanding presence among the various dock workers.

The two embraced each other in a warm hug.

"How have you been?" said Westley.

"I've had a fair share of adventures," said Jana.

"So I've heard," said Westley. "You were going to marry Tybilt? And then you killed a dragon? Sounds like a busy time of it."

"Yes," said Jana, "busy is one way to describe it. How have you been?"

"Things have been good here," said Westley, "good for the shipping business. Trade's loosened up a bit since we won, and it's been a boon for people who are willing to move things for pay. Last summer I was able to quit the boat entirely and stay on land to manage things."

"Oh really?" said Jana. "I didn't think anything could take the sea out of you."

"Well," said Westley, "it's not out of me entirely. Every once in a while I take a small boat out in the middle of the night for a sort of pleasure cruise. I love how the harbor looks in the moonlight."

"Such a sentimentalist you are," said Jana.

"Well," said Westley, "I'm now in charge of five boats. It's a lot to keep track of."

"Five boats?" said Jana. "That's a lot."

"I'd like to make it six," said Westley. "Perhaps later this summer."

"I don't suppose you'd have one of those boats free," said Jana.

"Free?" said Westley. "What for?"

"There's an island I need to get to," said Jana. "I could use your help."

"Anything I can do," said Westley. "I owe you one."

"Ever hear of the Cuttyhunk Islands?" said Jana.

"Sure have," said Westley.

"I need to go there," said Jana.

"It'll never happen," said Westley.

"No?" said Jana.

"That's a myth," said Westley. "I know one guy who was convinced that the Cuttyhunk Isles were the source of great riches and prosperity and all he talked about was when he got a boat of his own he was going to find them. He searched for them for two years straight before coming back here, only to die of scurvy. They don't exist, and you're better off never looking for them."

"They do exist," said Jana.

"What makes you so sure?" said Westley.

"They are protected by magic," said Jana. "Nobody would ever be able to find them through normal means, no matter how hard they looked. I know of many different spells that do the same thing on a smaller scale. I know that I'll be able to find the islands if I can get close."

"You really think so?" said Westley. "What's so important there anyway? Eternal youth? Riches beyond your wildest dreams?"

"Not quite," said Jana.

"All right," said Westley. "I've heard some pretty impressive stories about what's out there. Tell me yours."

"The islands are magic," said Jana.

"What do you mean by that?" said Westley.

"As I understand it," said Jana, "and I've never been there so I can only rely on what I've heard, the islands split off from the mainland over five thousand years ago, when magic was still abundant and the existing society was able to do pretty remarkable things with it. You see that spire? They did that with magic."

Jana pointed to the Noonmark spire, which hung over the city of Hockessin directly to the south. It was a tall jut of black rock, stretched impossibly over the edge of the canyon wall. The color of the mountain contrasted sharply with the light grey of the canyon walls. The mountain itself seemed out of place on the gently rolling plains at the top of the canyon and for miles south and west of it.

"Magic, you say," said Westley.

"On that island are magical creatures," said Jana. "The way magic works is that magical creatures emit an energy that can be drawn from and shaped or transformed or simply used to do miraculous things. You've seen me conjure a fireball in my hand, right? I'm using that energy to do that."

"So there's magical energy on that island?" said Westley.

"Yes," said Jana, "in an amount orders of magnitude more powerful than we have here. Most of the energy I can use here is emitted by one of nine ancient dragons that roam the land. On that island, there are thousands of magical creatures. I've felt what it's like to stand next to an ancient dragon. The power available is overwhelming; it was how I was able to defeat one of them. On those islands, the power is even stronger."

Westley laughed. "Suppose I believed you," he said, "which I don't... not yet. What would you do with it? Shoot some fireworks off on the island?"

"I'd bring it back," said Jana.

Westley laughed loudly.

"There is an insect living there called the flutterbee," said Jana. "If we can bring a flutterbee hive back to the mainland, they can repopulate the plains and bring the magic back to this land."

Westley laughed again. "That sounds preposterous," he said. "That's the silliest idea I've heard since, well..."

"Since someone suggested that we get Westvalian troops out of Hockessin by throwing tomatoes at them?" asked Jana.

Jamie smiled. She remembered doing that.

Westley's laugh died down. He put his hands on his hips and looked at Jana.

"You're serious, aren't you?" he asked.

"The ancient dragon Kaseraak has asked me to do this," Jana said. "Apparently they need the flutterbees to procreate. If I don't do this, it's possible magic will die."

"Hm, okay," said Westley, "let me think."

Jana tapped her foot.

"The fishing boat Vengeance is due to return tomorrow," said Westley. "It's one of my smaller boats, but it should be large enough for you. I think I can let you take that."

"I want you to come with me," said Jana.

"I can't," said Westley.

"You can," said Jana. "I need you. I have no idea how to sail a ship."

"I have all the account records to go through," said Westley, "and the manifest reports, and the sail logs. It's not easy handling five ships."

"What are you, a sailor or an accountant?" asked Jana.

"This is what I do," said Westley. "I'm too old to sail."

"The hell you are," said Jana. "Come on, come on one last adventure with me. I need you."

Westley sighed and thought about it for a moment. "I do owe you one," he said.

Jamie clapped. "All right," she said.

"Okay," said Westley, "I'll come with you. If only to see what in the world a flutterbee is."

"Excellent," said Jana.

"The boat should be in the harbor in the morning," said Westley, "and with all luck it should be ready to go a couple days from now. What sort of crew will you be needing?"

"As small as possible," said Jana. "I figure magic can handle the heavy lifting and when we get there people we don't know might become liabilities."

"All right then," said Westley. "I'll get two good men for you, and we should be set."

"I'm hoping to bring two other people along," said Jana, "making seven of us in total."

"Sounds good," said Westley.

Fifteen minutes later Jana and Jamie were on their way to find their next recruit: Mallory Greene. That took them to the northwestern part of Hockessin, where they stood at the door of Buckley's Tavern.

"Stick close to me, Jamie," Jana said. "People in here aren't likely to take kindly to someone your age."

"I'm thirteen," Jamie said defiantly.

"My point exactly," said Jana.

Jana opened the door to the tavern and a gust of black smoke blew out.

Buckley's Tavern was not the worst tavern in Hockessin, at least not in the sense that "worst" meant bad. But it certainly was a prototype of the sort; if one wished to go to a "bad" tavern, Buckley's would be a pretty good choice.

The stench of the place overwhelmed Jamie as she entered. It was a mixture of different things that she couldn't quite identify. Some of it was the smoke from pipes that any number of rough people had in their mouths, and not all of them were smoking variants of the same plant. Some of it was the odor of cheap liquor that had been spilled on most of the surfaces and some of the people in the tavern. Some of it was the sweat of the people, perhaps fifty or sixty squeezed into a building twenty feet to a side. Some of it was the smoke from a meat of some sort roasting over a fire pit in the back half of the tavern.

Jamie coughed. Jana looked through the crowd. A moment later she saw what she was looking for: a group of people playing darts. She made their way over there just in time to hear the thunk of a dart against a board.

"18!" said a young man. Jamie guessed that he was probably a sailor from his build and dress, though a young one. He only had one tattoo, from what Jamie could see.

"Not bad," said a small woman from behind him. "I might have miscalculated on our wager. Seems I underestimated you."

"You're not getting out of this now," the man said. "Five of my buddies here saw you make that bet. You have nowhere to run."

"Fair's fair," said the woman. "Looks like I'll be owing you fifty silver. Down by fifty-eight with one dart left, not much hope for me."

"You've lost your touch," said the young man. "The game's up. You've lost."

"Perhaps I have," she said. "Perhaps I haven't. Maybe you'd like to make it more interesting."

"Fifty silver is plenty interesting for me," the young man said.

"Double it," said the woman, "and I'll take my last shot blindfolded."

The young man laughed. "So eager to give away your gold? You probably have some trick or something."

"No tricks," said the woman. "And that woman there will see to it that there's no trickery."

The woman pointed directly at Jana. Jana nodded and pushed her way over to the group.

"Here," said the woman as she held up a leather blindfold, "put this on me."

"Hey," said the young man, "what are you trying to pull? That's some kind of trick blindfold?"

"No," the woman said with a sigh, "here, look at it if you want. Or find something of your own. It doesn't matter to me."

The young man took the blindfold and looked at it. He put it up to his eyes as if to attempt to look through it. A moment later, he nodded, satisfied that the blindfold was legitimate.

"Put it on yourself, if you like," said the woman.

The woman flipped up her long blue hair and looked out toward the dartboard. As the young man began to tie the blindfold on to the woman, Jana knelt over toward Jamie to whisper in her ear.

"That young man is about to learn a very expensive lesson," said Jana.

"What?" said Jamie softly. "She has to hit triple-20 blindfolded. That's impossible."

The young woman lifted up her dart and appeared to wobble for a moment. She steadied herself and then took aim.

"No," whispered Jana, "it's a sucker bet. If she couldn't do it…"

The woman tossed the dart at the dartboard. It hit the board with a loud thunk.

"…she wouldn't suggest the bet," said Jana.

The young man looked at the board, his jaw agape. He had just lost a hundred silver.

"Pay up," said the woman with a grin as she took off her blindfold.

"I don't believe it!" the young man said. "It must have been some kind of trick."

"It wasn't a trick," the woman said. "You lost. Pay up."

"Like hell I will," said the young man. "I've got five of my sailor friends here. Who do you have? Who's going to make me?"

"A pity," said the young woman. "I thought you might say that. It's why I took the liberty of relieving you of your coin purse when you put the blindfold on me."

"Hey!" said the young man as he patted by his belt, realizing that she was right. "Thief! Get her, boys!"

The young man swung his hand clumsily in an attempt to punch the woman. The woman ducked out of the way and made her way behind Jana. Jana took a step in front of her to protect her.

"Out of my way, Red," said the young man. "That witch stole a week's pay, and I'll bust up anyone who gets in my way."

"With respect, little boy," Jana said, "you are out of your league."

The young man again threw a punch, this time at Jana. Jana snapped her fingers, and a moment later his fist barreled into his own stomach. He doubled over in pain.

The other five men the young man was with took one look at Jana and made for the door. Jana let them go.

"You see," Jana said. "You've made a horrible mistake. The woman you were playing darts against? That's Mallory Greene. The Mallory Greene. The one who can shoot a hummingbird from sixty paces with a long bow. Playing darts with her is a sucker's game, and you're the sucker."

"And the woman you just threw a punch at?" said Mallory. "That's Jana Aliston. The Jana Aliston. The dragon slayer. Throwing a punch at her is like signing your own death warrant."

"So," said Jana, "I suggest you leave this place."

"And never return," said Mallory.

The young man did as they suggested. He really didn't have a choice, not if he wanted to live.

"So how have you been?" Jana asked Mallory when the three found a corner of the tavern to call their own.

"Good!" said Mallory. "Been doing all sorts of stuff, tracking, hunting, all over. I like to come back here regularly for the darts."

"I figured I'd find you here," said Jana.

"Poor guy there really didn't have a chance," said Mallory. "I spotted him a hundred points, and it didn't matter. I could have beaten him by a lot but I figured I'd play him to the last dart."

"Get in a good sucker bet," said Jana.

"What's a sucker bet?" asked Jamie.

"I told you that before," said Jana.

"It's when you lure someone into betting more than they might otherwise by pretending to not be as good as you are," said Mallory. "He thought he had a chance to beat me, because the game before I was flinging darts all over the place and only won by two. That's the trick to this game. Never win by a lot. Nobody will play against you that way."

Jana nodded. "I'd never play against you," she said.

"Not even just for fun?" said Mallory.

"Heh," Jana said, "what fun would that be? Going in to know I'd lose."

"What if you used magic?" asked Jamie.

"There's a thought," said Jana. "Probably not even then, though. Mallory's played darts for years. I barely know the rules."

"So what brings you to Hockessin?" said Mallory.

"Adventure," said Jana.

"Need a hand?" asked Mallory.

"I was hoping for one," said Jana.

"Count me in," said Mallory. "I've got nothing going on where they won't miss me."

"We'd be sailing to the Cuttyhunk Islands," said Jana, "to acquire a flutterbee hive."

"Sounds great," said Mallory. "When are you setting off?"

"Wait," said Jamie. "You know about the islands? Or about the flutterbees?"

"Nah," said Mallory. "I don't care. It just sounds good."

"We'd be looking to set sail the morning after tomorrow," Jana said. "Bring your gear."

"Wouldn't have it any other way," said Mallory. "Sure you don't want to play a round of darts? Just for fun?"

"Okay," said Jana, "just one."

Three hours, six rounds of darts and one surprisingly tasty meal later, Jamie and Jana left the tavern. They were laughing over the stories told, and looking forward to their coming adventure.

"One more to go," said Jana.

"Anna?" asked Jamie.

"Right," said Jana. "I'm worried most about her."

"She's your sister," said Jamie.

"She is that," said Jana. "But she's notorious for not wanting to take action or go on an adventure. She likes the safety of a town and generally only uses magic for research. Getting her to help the revolution in Hockessin was tough. Some of the fights she wasn't up for. Remember?"

"I remember," said Jamie. Jamie knew that once Anna was unable to help Jana defend Sycosina against a large number of Westvalian troops.

"She might like this," said Jana. "She might not. One other thing to consider is that she's on lead committee for running Hockessin. She's likely to be quite busy."

"Yes," said Jamie. "She was quite involved in it the last time we saw her."

"I don't have high hopes," said Jana. "I think we have a one in three shot. But I really want her to come."

"So tell her that," said Jamie.

"Oh, I will. Believe me, I will."

Jana and Jamie walked toward Anna's residence. Jamie knew it as a place where Anna not only lived, but also kept an office for consulting with Hockessin's residence. The office was in the front part of the building; Anna's residence was in the back. Jana and Jamie made their way to the back.

Jana knocked. The door opened after about ten seconds.

"Sis!" said Anna.

"Hey there, Anna," said Jana with a smile.

Anna Aliston cut an impressive figure. She was five and three-quarters feet tall, with a strong but not large frame. She had broad shoulders like Jana, but a thinner waist and trimmer legs. Her hair was a deeper red, more crimson as compared to the fire of Jana's hair. She would command the attention of almost any room, as long as she were not standing next to her sister.

Jamie and Jana were invited inside. The three sat in the room and caught up. Anna had heard rumors of what Jana had been up to since the last time she saw her, which was at Jana's failed wedding ceremony. She asked if Jana had really killed a dragon, and Jana told her that story. She expressed surprise that she seemed to still be on good terms with Tybilt, and that Sycosina had not yet destroyed the facade of the fight at the end of the wedding, and Westvalian society for that matter. Jana laughed.

All of this had seemed familiar to Jamie, but hearing Jana retelling the stories for Anna made them seem grander in some way. Jamie had played a part in downing an ancient dragon, and until this point she hadn't realized how momentous an occasion it was. The wedding also seemed like a world changing event, at least as how Jana told it.

Anna told Jana of her life in Hockessin, which was mundane both in comparison and probably by itself. The city had recovered well during its newly granted freedom from Westvalia, and seemed to once again be becoming the hub of the Eastern Lands. There were many visitors and many new immigrants, and Anna was in charge of it all, at least in part. It was a happy time to be living in Hockessin.

"So what brings you to town?" asked Anna after the catching up wound down.

"We have a mission," said Jana.

"A mission?" asked Anna. "From Tybilt, again?"

"No," said Jana. "This one is for the ancient dragons."

"Ancient dragons?" said Anna. "You just killed one of them. Why would you do anything for them?"

"It's a complicated thing," said Jana.

"It might avert a war," said Jamie.

"Ah," said Anna. "I see."

"Let me explain," said Jana.

Jana explained to Anna how Kaseraak had arrived in Westvalia to look for her. She explained the proposition Kaseraak had put to her: acquire a hive of flutterbees or face war between the ancient dragons and humanity. She explained how she called that bluff, and learned the reasons why the ancient dragons wanted the flutterbees in the first place. She explained the origin of the island, the presumed existence of the Vaspen tribe, and the dangers that faced them.

"So what do you get out of it?" asked Anna.

"Magic," said Jana. "We put flutterbees back in Westvalia, we will have a source of magic. That source will remain there even if, for whatever reason, the ancient dragons end up dying out. It will make magic much more powerful, and will likely make it a permanent fixture in the power structure of the land."

"I don't know," said Anna.

"I've learned quite a few things in studying to face Norzakind," said Jana. "One of the things I've learned is that there's a reason for most every unusual geographic feature in the land. As preposterous as it sounds now, it was magic that did it. Magic created the Noonmark Spire."

"And you think you'll be able to be that powerful again?" asked Anna.

"Maybe," said Jana. "Maybe not for me. Maybe for Jamie. Maybe whoever becomes Jamie's apprentice. We have a chance to change the world."

"I'm sure," said Anna with a half sneer. She was never much of one for world-changing events.

"I want you to help us," said Jana.

"Impossible," said Anna.

"It's not impossible," said Jana.

"We have a legislative session in two weeks," said Anna. "This is the busiest time of year for me. I have responsibilities to Hockessin."

"This is a once-in-a-lifetime opportunity, Anna."

"I can't," said Anna, "there's no way I could just up and leave, even if I wanted to. Which I don't. You all are going to get yourself killed down there."

"That's why I need you," said Jana.

"Jana, sis, I can't," said Anna.

"Well, I guess that's that, then," said Jana.

"What, that's it?" said Jamie.

"She doesn't want to go," said Jana. "She doesn't want to see what that magic would be like. Or study a flutterbee. I would have thought that would have sounded interesting."

"It is," said Anna, "I just have my responsibilities here."

"Consider your greater responsibilities," said Jana. "You're a mage, Anna. Have you forgotten after all this time?"

"No," said Anna. "That's why I sit on the council."

"This is about restoring magic," said Jana. "Restoring it to its rightful place in the order of things. That should mean something to you as a mage."

"It does," said Anna, "it does. And I'm very interested in it, really I am. But it's too dangerous, and…"

"It will be more dangerous with just one of us," said Jana. "Come on, sis, I really will need your help here. I don't think I can do this alone."

"You're just saying that," said Anna.

"I don't know what we'll be coming up against," said Jana. "Powerful mages, no doubt. I'd like to have someone else who can watch my back."

"Someone else?" said Jamie.

"Besides you," said Jana.

"Jana, I can't," said Anna. "Really, I'd like to, but they need me here."

"I need you, sis."

Anna thought about it for about ten seconds.

"Really?" she asked.

"Really," said Jana. "Just like when we freed Hockessin. I couldn't do that without you."

"Really," said Jamie.

Anna sighed. "I suppose I could resign my seat from the council."

"That's the spirit!" said Jana.

"Ah," said Anna, "I was tired of being on the council anyway. You know what happened to me today? Some guy came in complaining about the smell of fish near where he lived. This is a guy who lives two blocks from the harbor. What goes through these people's minds I don't know. Hey, don't like the smell of fish? Move to Bracken. Or Chuckston. Or Saston. This is a fishing town."

Jana and Jamie laughed.

"That's not the worst of it," said Anna. "Sometimes you get the time-crazies. These are the people who are absolutely obsessed with tracking time. They want to paint numbers all over the town saying when and where and what time the shadow of the spire will be. I mean, I think it's great for having a general sense for what time it is but there's a limit. It's become an obsession with some people."

"Sounds like it's time for a change," said Jana.

"Yeah, I think so," said Anna. "I think Hockessin's on it's feet now. It'll do fine without me."

"Great!" said Jana. "We're leaving the morning after tomorrow."

"I'll be there," said Anna.

Chapter Five

Sailing Away

The morning after tomorrow came quickly for Jamie. There were a lot of preparations necessary. The boat had to be cleaned, and provisions had to be loaded. The sails needed some minor repairs. In the end these things took care of themselves and the morning after tomorrow they were ready to go.

The crew totaled seven: Westley was the captain of the boat and had the command when the boat was at sea. Westley had two "hands", or assistants, one named Jay and the other Dea. He had told Jana that the two were reasonably trustworthy and experienced, and also knew their way with a sword if the need arose. Then there was Mallory, the boisterous petite hunter who stood not quite as tall as Jamie. Jana, Jamie and Anna rounded out the crew.

"Where to?" said Westley to Jana as the ship sailed out of harbor.

"The South Seas," said Jana. "Bisconty Bay."

The question was a formality and somewhat of a tradition. The day before Westley and Jana had plotted a course, so Westley knew very well where they were going and how they were to get there. It was as much a benefit to the others that he asked the question as it was for his own purposes.

The boat sailed within sight of the coastline for most of the trip. Jana explained to Jamie that the high seas could be rough, and that it was generally a good idea to remain in sight of the coast. Westley knew how to navigate a boat on the open seas but it was less preferable, especially since they didn't need to.

Jamie had never been on a boat before. She found the experience thrilling in many different ways. The floor of the boat rocked back and forth with the waves, an experience she had expected but couldn't have known before the trip. What she didn't expect was the sky at night. She had lived in the city of Westvalia for long enough now that she had gotten used to the smoke and the lights of the city obscuring the stars. Out in the open, the stars lit up the sky brilliantly, more so than she could remember in her rural home. She could find patterns in the sky she had never noticed before.

As she lay back against the bow deck of the boat, she told Jana of her surprise at how bright the stars were.

"Yes," said Jana. "They're the guides for the sailors."

"Guides?" said Jamie. "What do you mean?"

"Well," said Jana, "as I understand it the stars rotate in the sky according to a fixed pattern. If you know what to look for, you can tell which way is which, what time of day it is, and all sorts of other things. They can tell you how close you are to your destination, and things like that."

"Can you do that?" asked Jamie.

"No," said Jana. "At my best I can recognize a couple patterns, like a hunter or a dog. But I bet Westley and his two hands can both do it. Go ask them how much further we have to go."

"Okay," said Jamie.

Jamie walked down to the center of the boat where Westley was relaxing. She asked him how much further they had to go.

"A couple hundred miles still," said Westley. "If the wind holds, we should be to the bay in three days. After that, it's up to Jana. Nobody knows where the islands are."

Jamie nodded. She went back up to Jana and lay back to look at the stars. She had a fun time connecting the stars together to make patterns, and she thought she could make out a hunter and his dogs. But beyond that she didn't know anything more about them.

Three days later in the afternoon the boat had reached Bisconty Bay and the small town of Bisconty. The bay was a small one, perhaps five miles wide, with the town located in the center of the circular shore. The crew went ashore for a night and returned to the boat the next morning. Jana gave the order for Westley to sail south.

"Due south," said Jana.

"We'll be out of sight of land in a few hours," said Westley. "After that I won't have any reference points."

"If what I know about the islands is true," said Jana, "Anna and I should be able to detect the magic from a ways away. We just need to get close."

"I'll get you close," said Westley.

The crew sailed south. As Westley said, the land retreated over the horizon to the north, and all Jamie could see was the soft blue of the South Sea. The waves began to get stronger, and the boat bobbed a bit higher with each passing one.

Jamie looked out over the horizon to the south. On Westley's suggestion, she climbed to the top of the larger mast of the boat, the one that held two square sails. She looked out and could see nothing but blue seas. In a very real sense, she had lost herself in the ocean. She had no idea where she was going until she asked Westley about it.

"This is a trick my dad taught me," Westley said. "All it requires is a stick that's one foot long and a sunny day and a bit of knowledge of what season it is. The key starting point is to know how long of a shadow the stick casts at noon. That's going to differ as you go from place to place, but it's generally going to be shorter the further south you go, and it's going to be shorter the closer you are to summer."

"Let's take this now," said Westley. "Right now I know that this stick casts a shadow three quarters of a foot long at noon. I put it down and I see that the shadow is a foot and three quarters long. A foot and three quarters minus three quarters a foot is one. I take that number, and add one to it to get two. Next, I divide six by that number. It's six because it's early spring or early autumn. It would be seven for late spring and mid-summer, and five for late autumn or mid-winter. Six divided by two is three. That's how many hours it is until sunset. In the morning it would be how many hours it was since the sun rose. Since the sun sets at about six o'clock in the early spring, I now know it's three o'clock."

"Once we know that it's three o'clock, we can figure out the direction," said Westley. "As everyone in Hockessin knows, shadows point due north at noon. At six in the morning, they point west, at nine, northwest, at three northeast and at six east. Since it's three o'clock now, we know that the shadow is pointing northeast, and thus south is that way."

Westley pointed toward the front of the boat, toward an expanse of sea that looked to Jamie like any other expanse of sea. Jamie was fascinated to watch the demonstration, and later learned that Westley had much finer equipment that he used to make the measurement more exact. On the open seas, Westley explained, it was the only way to make sure you weren't sailing in circles. The winds generally came from the west this time of year, but the winds were not reliable.

Jamie listened intently to the instructions Westley gave her. She knew that she would have difficulty understanding it; subtracting one half from one and a half and dividing six by two were things that generally had no place in the farm where she grew up, nor in her training with Jana as a mage. She had rarely needed math skills beyond simple counting, so the formula for finding the time of day confused her quite a bit. But she understood the basic gist of the method: the more time it was until or since noon, the longer an object's shadow would be.

At night, Westley explained, the job of determining a direction was much easier. The stars to the north stayed the same throughout the year, and there were a pair of stars that basically straddled the north pole. If you could find those, you would know which direction was north. Jamie picked that up rather quickly, far more quickly than the bit with the stick and the shadow during the daytime.

It was the evening of the second day out of Port Bisconty that Jamie sensed something weird in the air. It took her a little time to recognize what it was. It was magic. Normally there would be a set amount of magic in the air from which Jamie could draw to cast her spells. That amount didn't vary much, except when she was close to an ancient dragon. That evening, it started to feel as it did when she was close to Kaseraak. Magic was becoming more powerful.

"We're close!" said Jamie.

"I know," said Jana.

"Okay," said Westley. "I've gotten us this far. Where to now?"

"I don't know," said Jana. "The magic's strong, and I think what would best make sense is to go to where it's stronger. If we can zero in on where it's strongest I think we'll find it."

"Mallory," said Westley, "climb the mast and see if you can see anything."

Mallory climbed up the mainsail and looked out over the horizon. All she could see was the sea.

"Nothing," said Mallory.

"We can try that for a little bit," said Westley. "But it would work better if we could have some sense of direction. The wind only goes one way, and it's tough to sail into it."

"I understand," said Jana. "But I don't know what else to do."

The boat sailed for a couple hours. Three times, Jana asked Westley to change course. Ten minutes after the third course change, Jana sighed in exasperation.

"There's too much variance," said Jana. "I'm trying to find a general pattern but there's just too much noise. We'll never find it this way."

"There has to be a way," said Westley.

"If I could uncover the spell used to hide the islands," said Jana, "that might lead us in the right direction, but I don't know where to start with that. The magic's so much more powerful than what I'm used to dealing with that I wouldn't know how to crack it."

"Just try your best," said Westley.

Jana concentrated for several minutes, but nothing seemed to come from it. Suddenly Anna walked toward the bow of the boat. She moved as one who had noticed something. Jamie followed her.

"What is it?" asked Jamie.

"The Wolf's Paw," said Anna.

"The what?" asked Jamie. Anna's statement had caught the attention of Westley; the ship's captain jumped up toward Anna.

"What about it?" said Westley.

"Look," said Anna, pointing to the horizon forward and to the right of the boat.

Jamie looked at the stars. She had a very basic understanding of the constellations, and so she knew what the Wolf constellation looked like. It had a few moderately bright stars forming a box of a body, a clump of stars forming its head, and two relatively bright stars forming its paws. One star in particular, a yellow-orangish one off the right side of the constellation, was one of the thirty brightest stars in the sky. It had become known as the Wolf's Paw.

Jamie knew that at this time of year, the Wolf was in the western skies. She looked to the constellation and found it. When she looked at the paw, she noticed something odd: there were two Wolf's Paws.

"There are two of them!" said Jamie.

"Yes," said Anna. "I bet that whatever magic it is that makes these islands undetectable also does some strange things to the sky. I would lay pretty heavy odds that our island is in that direction."

"Brilliant!" said Westley. "Jay," he continued, calling to one of the hands, "steer us toward the Wolf's Paw."

"Aye, captain," Jay said.

Jamie felt a twinge of excitement as the boat turned to the right and sailed to the twin stars. She felt as though they were on the verge of something big.

As the boat sailed onwards, the appearance of the star began to change. At first, it collapsed to a single star, making Jamie wonder if the first sighting was a shared hallucination. A few minutes later, the star split into four. It then collapsed again, and at one point completely disappeared. Then it got brighter and brighter.

"We're close," said Jana. "I can feel it. The magic is really…"

Jana's words were interrupted by a loud and ugly scraping noise underneath the boat.

"We've hit something!" yelled Dea.

A split second later a large cliff appeared before the ship. It was impossibly tall and impossibly close.

"Hard to port!" yelled Westley, but it was too late. The boat turned to the left. A hard wave pounded the boat's left side, and a loud crash sounded from the right. Wood below deck splintered, and the right side of the boat looked like it would collapse in too. Jamie lost her balance and fell. She then grabbed for a railing, a rope, anything she could to steady herself as the boat tipped over to the right. The wooden beams of the boat cracked underneath.

After twenty seconds of crunching and cracking, the boat finally came to a rest, nearly upright. Most of the deck had survived the crash, though a small portion about four yards long and one yard wide on the right side had collapsed downward. The damage below was far more extensive. Large dark rock jutted through the boat, and below deck the boat was littered with splinters and sticks of wood.

"I think we're safe here for the night," said Jana. "We seem to be stuck."

"I'll say," said Jay.

"What are we going to do?" said Westley. "We can't repair that. There's no way we'll be able to sail off of here, wherever here is. We're trapped."

"Calm down," said Mallory.

"We'll figure something out," said Anna. "But we need light to see what situation we're in."

"Let's just try to get some rest for the night," said Jana, "and hope the waves don't wash us out to sea."

"We're pretty stuck," said Jay.

"That's the best we can do for now," said Jana.

It sure seemed like that to Jamie. They weren't going anywhere.

Chapter Six

The Island

Jamie woke up the next morning after a rough night's sleep. She could only barely put aside her fear that the boat would detach from the rocks upon which it was perched and sink into the cove. But she had slept once on the cold floor of a Westvalian prison before, once in the collapsed remains of a wooden building in Jimburgh, and countless times in the open in the wilderness. Sleeping in odd places was something she had gotten used to by now.

The morning sun gave the crew their first good look at their surroundings. The boat was wrecked in a small cove that was about five hundred yards wide, stretching from a ridge south of the boat and arcing around to another ridge to the northwest. The boat was toward the southern end of the cove, perhaps a hundred yards from the southern ridge. The coast of the island was rocky, save for a beach about ten feet deep running along the inside of the cove. From the beach a cliff rose sharply up to the main part of the island between twenty and twenty-five feet above the sea level. Jamie couldn't see what was up there.

The crew waded ashore to the beach. The beach was a steep one, and the back half of the sand was completely dry. Westley gave the orders to set up a camp toward the center of the beach. Jamie felt a chill as she walked closer to the rocks; the cliffs surrounding the cove were steep enough to block the morning sun from reaching the ground. For an island in the southern seas, it felt cold.

The magnitude of the wreck was apparent from the beach. A rock rose about two feet above the sea some twenty feet away from the beach. The boat was perched on the rock, with a hole about eight feet wide on its right side. Jamie looked at the boat and felt that it would never be able to sail again.

As Jamie watched the rest of the crew ferry supplies to the beach, she felt powerless. If only there were something she could do! But the boat was stuck, beyond repair. The cliffs bordering the cove were slick and dangerous. She could do nothing but sit there. To pass the time, she decided to draw in the sand.

She drew a picture from their earlier encounter with Norzakind. There was a time in that encounter where Jamie was certain that she was going to die. Sycosina had been rendered helpless, forced to confront the terror felt by an entire society as it faced its own fiery death. Jana was similarly rendered helpless, encased in a large block of ice. There was just the dragon and Jamie. Jamie remembered throwing fireballs madly at the dragon with no apparent effect. The dragon looked at her, opened her mouth, and doused her with her flames. Somehow, Jamie was able to throw up a shield powerful enough to protect her from the fire, but the effort was just barely sufficient. Jamie drew a picture of herself cowering before the dragon, waiting her fate.

Of course, the dragon didn't kill her. Jana freed herself from the block of ice and then with a mad fury, she defeated the dragon. After her initial drawing was done, Jamie drew several lines ferociously, erasing the drawing of the dragon from the sand. As her hand moved, she recalled the feeling of pride and wonder as Jana proved herself more powerful than the dragon.

"We can't just stay here," Jana said to no one in particular. The crew had gotten the supplies over, and there were now two makeshift tents in the shadow of the cove.

"Let's see if we can find a way up this cliff," said Anna.

Jamie watched for a moment as Jana, Anna, Mallory and Westley each searched the cliff for a foothold. Jamie again felt frustrated at not being able to help. She walked up the beach to the north and sat down. She started to draw again, but stopped after about thirty seconds. She didn't feel like drawing.

She remembered a game she played a while back at Sycosina's hut in the Midnight Woods. She would conjure a ball of fire and then see how far she could throw it. Sycosina's hut was in a large barren clearing, and Jamie had hoped that she would have been able to reach the edge of the clearing.

She looked at the ridge to the northwest. It was a few hundred yards away, further than the edge of Sycosina's clearing was. But Jamie had two years of practice since then, and besides, Jana had said the magic was more powerful on the island. She wondered whether she could do it.

Jamie took a deep breath and started the fireball spell. The first step was to collect magical energy into a small ball in her hand, enough to…

BANG.

Jamie's thoughts were interrupted by a loud explosion that knocked Jamie to the ground. Jamie shook her head and crawled onto her knees, wondering what had happened.

"Jamie!" yelled Jana.

Jana and Anna ran over to Jamie. After a momentary inspection revealed no serious injury, Jana helped Jamie to her feet.

"What were you doing?" said Jana.

"I was bored," said Jamie. "I wanted to see if I could hit that ridge with a fireball."

"You have to be very careful with magic here, sprite," Jana said. "It's so powerful that you're going to end up struggling to control some very basic things."

"Also," said Anna, "we don't know what's out there. I'm not sure if we want to advertise our presence here."

"But I'm bored," said Jamie. "I can't do anything."

"I know," said Jana. "I know it's frustrating. We can't do anything either. Those rocks are so slick from the sea mist that it's nearly impossible to climb them."

"And there doesn't seem to be any way around the cove to either side," said Anna. "We'd get pounded to death by the waves."

"I can't just sit around and do nothing," said Jamie.

"We'll figure something out, Jamie," said Jana. "Why don't you draw for a bit?"

"Okay," Jamie said, resigning herself to it.

Several years ago Jamie would have been thrilled to be told to go draw. Drawing was her one escape from a life of menial servitude, from her life of subsistence farmings in the impoverished plains east of Chuckston. Since that time a new world had opened up before her. She was being trained by Jana to be a mage. She had met kings and dragons and princesses and talking bears.

Jamie drew half-heartedly and let her mind wander as she did. She remembered a time when she used her magic to draw onto the surface of solid rock. Indeed, that was the very first thing Jana had taught her. With a mischievous grin, she stood up. Jana had told her to draw, but she didn't tell her how to draw. She never said she couldn't draw with magic.

Jamie remembered a spell she had learned a few years ago. It involved making magical energy swirl around in spirals. Jamie used the spell to dig a hole. Why not dig a trench here, Jamie thought. It would be one really big drawing.

Jamie pointed her hands to a spot in the sand in front of her feet. She collected the magical energy around her and commanded it to swirl in a spiral. The ground then exploded on her, and she fell back on the sand, some four feet away from where there was a sizeable hole.

"That didn't take much effort," Jamie said to herself as she stood back up and dusted herself off. She looked at the hole in the sand, and then back to the indentation she had left in the sand. It was a fair distance away.

As she looked back and forth between the two, a thought struck her.

"I flew," she said softly to herself.

She looked over excitedly at Jana. She and the others were still trying to climb the cliff. It looked as if Westley had gotten the furthest, but he couldn't have been more than six feet above the beach, with still fifteen feet to go before the top of the cliff.

Jamie was determined to get there first.

Jamie stood up straight. She pointed her hands down and let the magical energy push against the ground. She made a small hole in the ground beneath her, and the sand kicked up around her. She desperately tried to maintain focus as her feet lifted off the ground. She hovered higher and higher until she was about four feet off the ground. Then she stopped her spell and let herself drop back down to the ground.

She could do it. She had just proven that to herself. It was now just a matter of practice. She figured that she could push herself straight up. But could she do more than that?

Jamie started again. She pushed herself off the ground to a point where she was three feet up in the air. She then tried pushing herself to one side. It felt suddenly as though she had lost her balance, and though she tried her best to recover, her concentration broke and she fell over and down to the ground. But she was undeterred.

Her next attempt was largely the same. She tried to move to one side, fell over, and lost her concentration.

It was on her third try she had some success. As she was hovering, she spread her arms out to her side, like a bird. She felt the breeze through her hands, and imagined that she were riding on a cloud. Instead of standing straight up, she was now lying prone, with her stomach facing the sand. From this position, she discovered that she didn't have to exert as much effort to keep herself floating in the air. The air had more surface area against which to push. She twisted herself slightly to the left. The left part of her fell down a half a foot, but she was able to recover and balance herself again. She discovered that she could move to the left that way.

From then it was a matter of practice before she got the hang of it. Rotating her body one way allowed her to turn a particular direction. For going forward or backward, she just needed to redirect the magical energies to a spot behind her or in front of her, which was easy enough. If she wanted to go up, she would push against the ground a bit harder with the magic, and down would mean easing up.

After about ten minutes, she was convinced that she had it figured out. She looked back toward the cliff. She looked back at the others. None of them had appeared to notice her; they seemed to still be struggling to find a path up the cliff. Jamie smiled. She would show them how to get up the cliff.

She pushed herself up higher, and then over toward the cliff. As she passed from being over the beach to being over the cliff, she felt a twinge in her nerves. A mistake would have been very painful.

Now that she was above the top of the cliff, she could see the rest of the island. Directly above the cliff was a large field, with tall grass greener than Jamie had ever seen before. To the west was the main part of the island. It was a slight hill that rose up perhaps ninety feet above the top of the cliff several miles away. The field immediately above the cliff was a large one, but it gave way to a forest of trees perhaps a third of a mile to the west. Jamie couldn't see anyone or anything.

Jamie slowly and carefully descended to a landing spot about five feet away from the edge of the cliff. She then crawled over to the edge of the cliff and looked down. Jana was about fifteen feet below her.

"Need a little help down there?" Jamie called out to Jana.

Jana stumbled a bit and managed to catch herself. She then looked up at Jamie.

"How did you get up there?" she asked.

"I flew," said Jamie.

"That's impossible," said Anna. "Years of research showed that there wasn't…"

Anna's voice trailed off into the distance. Jana smiled broadly.

"Good going, sprite," Jana said. "Now come down here and teach us how to do it so we can get everyone up there."

Jamie smiled and jumped off the cliff, using magic to slow her fall to a soft landing on the beach below. She, Jana and Anna went over to the broad portion of the beach while Mallory and Westley stopped their efforts to climb up the cliff.

Teaching the spell to Jana and Anna was exciting for Jamie. Never before had she been in a position of having more knowledge than another person. Never before had she seen her mentor mess something up that Jamie had already mastered. Jamie laughed and smiled as she instructed Jana on the technique. After about an hour of practice, Jana, Anna and Jamie felt as though they had mastered the basics. Soon after, Jana, Anna and Jamie gathered at the top of the cliff to look out at the island.

"Now what?" Anna said.

"I don't see anyone, or anything," Jana said.

"No," said Anna.

"I don't think we would," Jana said. "I get the feeling that unless we're extremely lucky or extremely careful, they'll see us before we'll see them. I wonder if they know we're here."

"If there is anyone," Anna said. "No human's come back from this island alive. We don't know anything about the Vaspen."

"No," said Jana, "but I think it's smarter to assume that there will be something than there won't. I hope so. It may be the only hope of fixing our boat."

"Yeah, that," said Anna.

"I think we need to fill Westley and Mallory in on what's up here," said Jana. "They've been waiting patiently."

"Do you think we could carry them up here?" asked Jamie.

"We probably could," said Jana. "The magic's there."

The three flew down to the base of the cliff and met up with Westley and Mallory.

"We didn't see anyone," Jana informed the others. "There's a broad field, then some woods leading up to a hill. It's possible that whatever settlements there may be are on the other side of the hill. We don't know."

"We didn't see any flutterbees," said Jamie.

"But they're around," said Anna. "Something's around. Magic's so strong here I feel like…" Anna paused for a moment's thought. "I feel like I could fly."

Jamie laughed.

"Can we get up there?" Westley asked.

"I think we'll be able to carry you up there," said Jana.

"Let's leave Jay and Dea here to watch over the boat," Westley said. "Maybe they can figure a way to get it off the rock, or salvage something out of it. I doubt they'd be much good where we're going."

Jana nodded. "That sounds like a fair plan."

"Buckle up, sprite," said Mallory to Jamie. "We're going for a ride."

"Where to now?" asked Westley once the group had gotten to the top of the cliff.

"I guess we look for a flutterbee hive," said Jana.

"We have two priorities right now," said Anna. "Find a flutterbee hive and find a way off this island. Maybe that's by fixing the boat. Maybe that's by finding a new boat. Let's keep our options open."

"Are we going to remember how to get back here?" asked Jamie.

"Leave that to me," said Mallory. "It's what I'm good at."

"All right," said Jana. "I suppose the best thing to do is to go up to the top of this hill. The view from up there should let us figure out how to proceed."

The group started to cross the field toward the hill. About fifty yards of a walk in, Jamie ducked as a large insect buzzed by her. She turned her head and saw the insect hovering over a set of flowers. It looked like a fuzzy striped ball, a half inch in diameter, with wings sticking out its top.

"Look," said Jamie. "Have you ever seen something like that before?"

"No," said Jana. "I think you've found us a flutterbee."

It wasn't long before the group spotted a flutterbee hive. It stuck out slightly from the tall grass. It was a pile of dried mud, almost in the shape of a tree stump, sitting in a brown patch of the field. It was about four feet tall and three feet wide. Scattered throughout the hive were small holes. Jamie could see perhaps fifty or sixty flutterbees crawling in and out of the hive.

"So that's what one is," said Anna.

"How do we move it?" asked Westley. "Should I get a shovel?"

"No," said Jana. "You'd get stung badly, and it would probably be damaged beyond use. We need to move it magically, somehow. But how do we do it without getting stung?"

"Do it from far away?" said Mallory.

"Can you put the flutterbees to sleep?" said Jamie. She had seen both Jana and Anna cause people to fall asleep back in Westvalia.

"Perhaps," said Anna. "It would be tricky. I've never tried to sleep more than two things at once."

"You have a lot of magic to play with," said Jana.

"Right now that doesn't matter," said Westley. "If we could move the hive to the boat we still wouldn't be able to leave. We need to figure out some other way off this island first."

"Let's keep going," said Jana. "I'm betting there are hundreds of these hives on the island. I think we can let this one be for now."

The group trudged onwards up the hill. After about three minutes they entered a forest. The forest was unlike any Jamie had ever seen before. The trees were tall, but their branches were too far above the ground to reach. The leaves of the trees were bigger than any Jamie had ever seen, and there were far fewer leaves on the ground than Jamie would expect. Vines hung from the limbs of the trees and wrapped around the trunks of the trees.

The noises of the forest were also unfamiliar to Jamie. Long ago, she had been taught to be afraid of the forest. When she first met Jana, she was almost too scared to enter the forest. She had learned to overcome that fear, but she still had a memory of it.

This forest scared her slightly by its unfamiliarity. In absolute terms, the Midnight Woods were a far scarier place to be, as they were so dark that one could easily imagine an animal pouncing from the darkness without notice. This forest was relatively bright. The animal sounds, however, were quite a bit different. There were animals and insects and other things out in this forest that Jamie could only imagine. For a girl with an active imagination, it was a little bit scary.

As the group continued up the hill, Jamie spotted an animal, or at least she thought she did. Out of the corner of her eye, she saw an elongated mass of fur, about one foot in length and a couple inches wide. Most of it, she believed, was the animal's tail, a striped pattern that made the animal hard to spot in the first place. When Jamie turned her head to look directly at the animal, it disappeared.

"Do you see anything?" Jamie whispered softly to Mallory.

"I've seen a few animals," said Mallory, "but no people. I think we're still safe."

"I don't know," said Jamie. "I get the feeling we're being watched."

"It's probably just your imagination," said Mallory.

The group continued upward. After about an hour and a half of climbing, the forest started to thin out. After another half hour, the group had reached another field, this one more rocky than grassy. They had reached the top of the hill.

Jamie could see the entire island from the top of the hill. Behind her was the steeper part of the island. The top of the hill seemed to be on the eastern half of what was otherwise an oval island. In front of her, the land spread down for what looked to be about fifteen miles before ending in a broad sandy beach. Beyond the beach, Jamie could see two other islands in the distance.

Next to the beach seemed to be a village of some sort. There were huts or houses with brown roofs. Some of the buildings were rectangular, and others were circular. From her experience with villages in Westvalia, it looked to hold perhaps a hundred to a hundred fifty people.

Up the hill from the village were several plowed fields. These fields rivaled Westvalia's palace gardens. Each plot seemed perfectly tended to, and even from this distance Jamie could tell that there was some advanced irrigation system throughout the fields. Slightly further up the hill from the fields were orchards and pastures. Like the fields, the placing of the trees and fences displayed a meticulous sense of order.

Whoever had placed them obviously had no resistance from the elements in doing so.

"So that's a Vaspen village," Jana said.

"Seems friendly enough," said Anna.

"At least they know something about boats," said Westley. "If we're lucky we can figure out a way of fixing them."

Westley pointed to a small cove south of the beach. Floating in the cove were several vessels, but they were unlike any boat Jamie had seen before. Instead of having a single hull, the vessels were two long pylons, connected in a way Jamie couldn't tell. They were too far away, too far to see how they worked. It was only the broad triangular sail which identified them as boats.

"I sure hope they're friendly," said Jamie.

"How do we approach them?" asked Mallory. "I mean, will they even be able to speak to us?"

"Your guess is as good as mine," said Jana. "They've lived here for five thousand years. A lot can happen in that time."

"We really don't have any other hope," said Westley. "I don't see a way of getting home without their help."

"Not the way our boat is," said Mallory.

"Let's get going," said Jana. "If we meet up with them, follow my lead. They use magic; maybe we'll be able to communicate better on that basis."

The group started their way down the hill. After a minute, they found a worn dirt path that wound its way down the shallow incline back into the woods. Grateful for any guidance, the group followed it, hoping that it would lead them to some help.

After about ten minutes of walking, the forest opened up into a small clearing. The clearing was circular, in a way that reminded Jamie of Sycosina's circular clearing in the Midnight Woods. This clearing was not barren, though; it had short grasses and a few shrubs but no trees. Jamie's eyes were drawn to an object in the center of the clearing.

At first Jamie couldn't tell what it was. It looked like a frame sculpture of some sort, white curved surfaces connected together in a pattern Jamie didn't initially recognize. It was about five feet tall, and about seven feet long, with the height concentrated on the right side of the object. Toward the top of the object were two large holes, while on the left side rows of spikes of varying lengths spread up and down along two ridges. After a few seconds, Jamie blinked with a sudden realization of what it was.

It was the skull of an ancient dragon.

Her instincts screamed out at her to run. But she couldn't run. She found herself drawn to the skull with an irresistible curiosity. Jamie blinked as she saw that she wasn't the only one.

"What is this?" said Mallory.

"It's an ancient dragon," Jamie said with a certainty that surprised her.

Somewhere in the distance a twig broke. Jamie couldn't hear it, but Mallory could.

"Someone's here," Mallory said.

"Armor up!" said Jana, echoing the words her mentor had taught her.

Jamie pulled a shield of magical force over her. She worried for Westley and Mallory, hoping that Jana and Anna could protect them. The group stepped away from the skull and formed a protective circle.

"Which way?" asked Jana. The group rotated slowly, backs to each other, each scanning the woods for some sign of life.

"I don't know," said Mallory. "Quiet."

Somewhere, another twig snapped. This time Jamie heard it.

"Right there!" Jamie said, pointing to where the sound was.

Every one in the group turned to look where Jamie pointed. None of them could see anything there. As they looked in one direction, they completely failed to notice the large net that had appeared from the other direction.

The net knocked everyone down. Jamie found herself wedged between the ground and Westley's chest. She reached out for magical energy to try to get the net off of her, but couldn't find any. She couldn't concentrate for long enough to gather anything. She rolled over onto her back and looked over at Jana and Anna. Apparently they were having similar problems.

A shadowy figure approached from the side of the clearing. Jamie couldn't see it through the net, but it appeared human in form. The shadowy figure pointed at Jamie through the net.

"Sleep," it said.

Jamie thought that was an excellent idea.

Chapter Seven

Old Conflicts

Jamie awoke in a haze. She found herself lying uncomfortably on packed dirt. She shook her head and tried to remember what happened. After what seemed like an hour but was actually only about fifteen seconds, she remembered. They had been captured.

She sat up. It was dark. She couldn't see more than three feet in front of her. With her sight useless, she focused on her other senses. She could hear a gentle breathing several yards away from her. Someone was there with her.

"Jana?" Jamie whispered quietly.

"No," came the reply. "It's Mallory."

"Where are we?" asked Jamie.

"As near as I can figure," said Mallory, "we're in some sort of magical prison. It's hard to move, but when I get so far I am pushed back to my feet. It doesn't feel like a wall, just like someone pushing you back."

"Where are the others?" asked Jamie.

"Oh, they're here," Mallory said. "They're just knocked out still. I figure I woke up first because I'm the shortest; you waking up next fits that theory. I figure Westley will be next, then Anna, then finally Jana."

"What do we do?" asked Jamie.

"I don't know," said Mallory. "I don't know what they're planning to do with us. I can't imagine it will be all that pleasant."

Jamie sighed. She stood up slowly.

"How can you see anything?" said Jamie.

"My eyes are probably better than yours," said Mallory. "I've trained myself to notice details."

It was true, thought Jamie.

"Well," said Jamie, "let's see if I can get some light here."

Jamie calmed herself and tried to collect magical energy to create a simple light. As she tried, the spell went completely wrong. Magical energy collected to her hand and then spilled through her fingers. She couldn't focus on it long enough to gather anything significant, not even for a simple light.

"Doesn't work," said Jamie.

"I didn't think it would," said Mallory. "Whoever we're dealing with seems to have a method for dealing with magic."

"That makes sense," said Jamie. "From what I've heard, their entire society relies upon it."

"Yeah," said Mallory. "Hopefully Jana can figure a way around it. Otherwise we're just stuck here waiting for them to do whatever they want."

Jamie nodded, but she wasn't about to give up just yet. She stood up and walked three feet in front of her. She could sense something in front of her. Magical energy swirled about them, with a power Jamie had never seen before coming to the island. After focusing on it for half a minute, Jamie felt it pulsing rapidly, perhaps five times per second. She reached out her hand to touch it. Her hand was knocked back into her with the force of a mild slap on the wrist.

Jamie wondered if she could break it. She looked down at her own body. Her pendant was still there. This was a pendant Jamie made for herself two months ago. The centerpiece of the pendant was a small emerald. Jamie was very proud of it, because it was the first time Jana had let her empower something other than a topaz. It held a lot more magical energy than a topaz, but it emitted power only slightly more powerful than a topaz.

Jamie focused on the gem and tried to draw power only from the gem, avoiding the swirling magic in the air around her. It was difficult, but she could do it. She gathered that magical energy in a spot above her, focusing it tightly to create a light. A moment later, the area lit up.

What it lit up into didn't help Jamie much. It seemed to be the inside of a wooden building. Overhead was a thatched roof, perhaps seven feet above the ground. After a while she began to notice a soft flickering glow, as though gases were swirling around her. Jamie figured that this was the magical barrier that prevented her from leaving the room.

Three feet beyond the barrier, she could see a door. It seemed unobtainable.

"So your magic does work," said Mallory.

"Only a little bit," said Jamie. "I have to rely on my gems rather than the air around me. I don't have many gems to draw from, though, so I can only do simple things like this light. Maybe Jana can do more, but I doubt it. The magic in the air is so powerful here that it overwhelms what I'm used to."

"I hope she can," Mallory said.

"Me too," Jamie said.

About half an hour later, the entire group had woken up. As Mallory predicted, Westley woke up first, then Anna, and then finally Jana. Jamie explained to Jana the situation.

"It's a magical shield," said Jamie, "that pulses rapidly. Those pulses push you back into the center of the room. There's something in the shield that prevents me from gathering magical energy from the air, but I found that if I focus on my gems that I can draw energy from them. That's how I made this light."

"Good work, sprite," said Jana. "That may be the key to getting us out of here. But for now I want you to hide that. Turn the light off."

"Why?" said Jamie.

"I'm betting these Vaspen know how long their sleep spells will last," said Jana, "and they'll be here soon, too soon for me to figure out any escape plan. In that time I don't want them to figure out what these gems are. Chances are they don't know."

"Okay," said Jamie. A flick of her mind later, the light went off and they were engulfed in darkness again.

"The magical power that they're used to is so strong," said Jana, "that I bet they've never had cause to store any of it anywhere. Maybe we can use that to our advantage."

"I hope so," said Mallory.

Several minutes planned. Jamie wondered if there was anything she could do. She sat back down on the ground and hugged her knees. She was scared.

The door to the room opened, revealing the bright sunlight beyond the door. This surprised Jamie. She could have sworn it was nighttime.

A man and a woman stepped through the door. The woman snapped her fingers and a light appeared above the group's head, illuminating the room and matching the sunlight from beyond the door.

"Prisoners," the man said calmly. His accent was unlike any Jamie had ever heard before. There was a crispness to his voice, a pronunciation of each letter within the word as if it alone was a vital part of the whole. With one word he established a sense of command that rivaled Tybilt.

Jana stood up to look the man in the eye. He was shorter and thinner than Jana, and seemed to be much older as well. His head was almost completely bald and his eyes were wrinkled. There was, however, no slouch in his posture to betray his age. He seemed completely fit.

The woman stood about an inch shorter than the man. She had the darkest hair Jamie had ever seen, a pure black that rivaled the darkness of the night. The hair fell just beyond her shoulders with a slight curl. Her body was thin like the man's, with only the slightest hint of curves to identify her as a woman.

There was something about the two that seemed out-of-place to Jamie. They weren't human. Perhaps their arms were too long, or their bones too thin. They would have stood out in a Westvalian crowd.

"Do you have anything to say for yourselves?" said the woman.

Jamie looked to Jana. She wasn't about to take the lead.

"What would you have us say?" Jana said.

"You have disturbed the tomb of Vilandra," the man said. "The consequences for doing so are severe."

"We didn't know what that was!" said Jamie. "We just…"

Jana shot Jamie a look that quieted her in an instant. Jamie sulked again. She had done something wrong.

"Don't try to fool us," the man said. "We know that you are allies of the dragons."

"You do?" said Jana.

"Your appearance here has been foretold for some time," said the man. "The dragons had been unable to defeat us directly so they have sent surrogates."

"The dragons were trying to defeat you?" said Anna.

The woman laughed. "I see. Perhaps you have been duped by them. Perhaps the elders will see that as cause to grant leniency."

"What happened?" asked Jamie.

"They never told you?" said the man. "It doesn't matter if they did. Their version would be inaccurate. Here, let me tell you the truth."

Jamie sat back and looked up at the man.

"Five thousand years ago, our direct ancestors had a vision," the man said. "They had a vision of dragons invading and destroying every town, every village, and every piece of our society. The vision was unequivocal: the dragons would destroy Vaspen society."

"Vaspen and the dragons were at peace with each other at the time," the woman said. "Most of the Vaspen chose not to believe the prophecy. Those that did came to this island. We pushed the island away from the mainland and disguised it from the dragons."

"From time to time," said the man, "our ancestors followed the wings of birds to the mainland. Soon they revealed that the prophecies were true. The land lay in flames, our buildings, our crops, our very existence reduced to smoldering rubble, all at the hands of the dragons."

"Our ancestors had cast a powerful spell to disguise this island," said the woman. "At the time, our best chance for survival seemed to be to remain hidden from the dragons' wrath."

"Unfortunately," said the man, "the disguise was seen through. It is a weakness of magical disguises that the disguise itself uses magic which can be detected; the dragons may not be able to see the island, but from its alteration of magical flow, they can sense that something is here. Some four thousand years after our islands detached from the mainland, the dragons found us."

"We were prepared," said the woman. "Our ancestors were the ones who believed in the power of prophecies and put their faith in them. Our faith has only increased since then. Our prophets had foretold the invasion by five dragons, led by a dark one named Vilandra. We sent our archmages up the hill to greet them."

"The battle was not particularly close," said the man. "Our ancestors who remained on the mainland were passive in the face of the threat of dragons and never bothered to prepare defenses. We were different. The dragons were overconfident and paid the price."

"We have preserved the skull of Vilandra as a reminder and a warning," said the woman. "It is a reminder to us all to be vigilant against the threat of the dragons. It is also a reminder of the power of prophecy."

"Several years ago," said the man, "our prophets foretold something new. They told of a group of five, led by two women with red hair, who would come to this island from the seas. They were acting on behalf of the dragons who would destroy us. They would, if unopposed, disrupt our very culture."

"It seems," said the woman, "that you are the prophesized five."

"We have no intention of disrupting your culture," said Jana.

"But you are emissaries of the dragons, are you not?" said the man.

"In a way," said Jana. "They did ask me to come here. But we act from our own interests, not from theirs."

"The dragons are duplicitous," said the woman. "You could be lying to us now. You could be telling what you believe is the truth. Either way, you would be acting on their behalf, whether unwittingly or not."

"Six months ago," said Jana, "I killed a dragon. One of ten remaining. I act out of my own interests."

"And what is it you seek?" said the man.

"Five thousand years ago," said Jana, "when the dragons slaughtered your ancestors, they also destroyed the habitat of the flutterbee. That habitant has been restored since that time, but we have no flutterbees. We wish to take one flutterbee hive back to the mainland to repopulate the fields."

"What benefit would that be to you?" said the woman.

"Right now," said Jana, "the dragons are the mainland's only source of magic. Magic has become a power controlled by a select few, with abilities far weaker than even this prison. Our nation is in conflict with the dragons, and we desire a source of magic other than the dragons. As a mage, I do not want to be dependent on a source of power so duplicitous."

"I see," said the man. "And the dragons get nothing out of this? They are the only ones who know of this island. Why would they tell you of its location?"

"I don't know." said Jana.

Jamie opened her eyes and looked at Jana. The man looked at Jamie.

"You, young one," said the man, pointing to Jamie. "Why do the dragons want the flutterbee?"

"I don't know," said Jamie. She felt nervous under the man's gaze.

"You are lying," said the man.

"You will not improve your position through deceit," said the woman.

"We don't know," said Jana. "We only know what they told us, which is not necessarily the truth."

"What did they tell you, then?" asked the man.

"They said that they needed the flutterbee to procreate," said Jana. "They think that without the flutterbee, their species will not survive."

"I see," said the man. "And you do not believe them?"

"I don't think they told me everything," said Jana.

"What are your intentions should you succeed in your plan?" said the woman. "After you return to the mainland with a hive of flutterbees?"

"I don't know," said Jana. "That's too far in advance to plan."

"I see," said the man.

"The prophecies foretold of a group of five that would come to disrupt our society," said the woman. "They did not, however, foretell of the precise method of this disruption. The source of the disruption could easily be a hasty and ill-considered execution of each of you."

"As of this moment, however," said the man, "we consider you to be the agents of the dragons who asked you to come here, your own stated intentions irrelevant to that concern. You are enemies of the Vaspen, and we will treat you that way until we have cause to believe otherwise."

"We will be discussing your fate," said the woman. "We will return to you with our decision in a few days."

"Don't we have anything to say about that?" asked Jamie.

"No," said the man.

With that, the pair turned and walked out of the room. The door closed and a second later the light above their heads extinguished, bathing them once again in darkness.

"So now what do we do?" asked Jamie after five minutes had passed.

"I don't know about you," said Westley, "but I don't like the idea of waiting around for them to decide what the prophecies tell them to do about us."

"Who knows what they'll come up with?" said Mallory. "Whatever we do could hurt them whether we intend to do it or not."

"Fate is a tricky thing," said Anna.

"Let me see what we can do with our magic," said Jana. "Maybe we can get out of here."

"Then what?" said Anna. "It's not like we'll be able to get off this island anyway."

"We can figure that out once we've escaped this prison," said Jana.

"No," said Anna, "we need to have some plan before that. If we break out of here only to be spotted again, they'll just put us back in here, without our clothes this time, and we'll have agitated them into thinking we mean them harm."

"If they think we mean them harm by trying to escape their prison," said Westley, "they'll think that anyway and there's nothing we can do."

"I agree with Anna," said Mallory. "We need to have some plan for what to do once we're on the other side of that barrier."

"How can we plan?" said Jana. "There's so much we don't know. We don't know whether we're in the middle of their village or at some remote outpost or whatever."

"We need some general idea," said Anna. "How can we get off this island?"

"Having a plan to get off this island doesn't do much good if we can't get out of this prison," said Westley.

"Getting out of this prison doesn't do us much good unless we can get off the island," said Mallory.

"Stop," said Jana. "We can't keep arguing like this. We need to be together on this. Let's take this one step at a time."

"That's how you always do it," said Anna.

"It's done well for me so far," said Jana.

"Has it?" asked Anna.

A silence fell over the group. Jamie went off to a corner of the room and curled up into a little ball. She hated it when Anna and Jana argued. She hated arguments altogether. Discussions were fine but this was beyond a discussion. This was an argument.

"Let's take this one step at a time," said Jana. "The first step is figuring out whether we even can get out of this prison. The second step is actually doing it, if that's what we decide to do. The third step is figuring out how to get out of this village, if we can. And then we figure out how to get off this island."

"I saw some boats from the hill," said Westley. "They weren't like anything I had ever seen before."

"At least we know they have some," said Jana. "That's a start."

"So the plan is to steal a boat?" said Anna. "Do you really think we'll be able to do that?"

"Anna," said Jana, "if you can't contribute anything constructive…"

"It's not about being constructive," said Anna, "it's about being reasonable. It's like saying our plan depends on being able to jump off the Noonmark Spire and land in central Hockessin."

"Jamie showed that might be possible," said Westley.

"You know what I mean," said Anna. "We were captured so easily and with so little effort that I seriously doubt we'll be able to sneak out of here, much less steal a boat."

"So what would you have us do?" said Westley. "Stay here and await our fate?"

"Yes," said Anna.

"I don't like that," said Westley.

"I don't like that at all," said Jana.

"Our survival may depend on convincing these Vaspen we're not a threat to them," said Anna. "If we try to do anything that would harm them, they'll pound us down like we were dirt. What would they care?"

"They may do that to us anyway," said Jana, "even if we're not a threat. They don't like dragons, and they don't like us."

"I don't see any other choice," said Anna.

"Well," said Jana. "I'm going to see what our options are. Let me try to break through this prison."

"I don't think that's a good idea," said Anna.

"I think we need to know," said Jana.

"I do as well," said Westley.

"I think Jana's right," said Mallory. "I'm not sure it will do us any good but knowing is better than not knowing."

"Oh, fine," said Anna. "I just don't hope I'll say 'I told you so.'"

"If it gets to that, little sister," Jana said, "those may be your last words."

Anna sat down in the corner of the room opposite of Jamie. She was obviously sulking.

Jamie watched Jana as she closed her eyes. Jana gathered the magic from the twenty or so gems that adorned her clothing. Back in Westvalia, those gems would have permitted her to continue to cast fireballs for an hour without a ready source of magic. Jamie wondered what they would do now.

She didn't have much time to wonder. A few moments later she saw the magical barrier flicker madly. The air sparked with purple, green and yellow gases, each swirling rapidly around the room. The room began to fill with a slight mist with the smell of burning wood. After about forty seconds the sparks stopped.

"I can't do it," said Jana. "I can create an opening about the size of my head, maybe a bit longer, for about half a second. After that the energy just swirls right through it. It's too small for someone to fit through, and even if they could fit through it I wouldn't want to be there when the magic closed the opening. It might tear you apart."

"So we're stuck here," said Westley.

"I think so," said Jana. "Hope that makes you happy, Anna."

"I'm thrilled," said Anna sarcastically. "Thrilled to be here."

Jana let that comment go. Jamie figured that was the best course of action.

"Let's try to get some rest," said Westley.

"And hope for a miracle," said Mallory.

Jamie closed her eyes. She didn't know what time it was but it felt like a good time to sleep.

Chapter Eight

Sam

Jamie dreamt.

She was flying in the clouds above non-descript fields. Flying with her was a green dragon. Jamie was circling around the dragon. Occasionally the dragon would breathe fire at her. Occasionally she would send an arc of blue energy toward the dragon. None of it was intended to harm the other. They were playing tag.

Jamie knew she was dreaming, not because she was really trapped in a magical prison at the mysterious Cuttyhunk Isles, but because dragons would never do that. She would never be able to do that. It was a silly game, and mages and dragons didn't have time for silly games.

Jamie ducked into a cloud. She dreamt that the cloud felt like walking through a thick mist and a slight drizzle. She hid in the cloud from the dragon. She could feel the cool water against her face.

A second later she found herself swimming in a pond. The pond was in a green valley surrounded by snow-covered mountains. Jamie looked around. She was far from any land. She wasn't that good of a swimmer, but apparently she had gotten here. In the distance she saw a white dragon. It was circling about and avoiding blasts of fire. Jamie tried to lift herself out of the pond but couldn't. She couldn't help. She couldn't do anything. She splashed the water helplessly.

"Hi there," came a voice out of nowhere. Jamie didn't recognize it. She looked around and couldn't see anyone, but then realized that she was dreaming and it was probably someone back in her real world talking to her.

She woke up and blinked. She rubbed her eyes to try to figure out who it was. It was pointless. The room was still dark.

"What's your name?" came the voice. The voice sounded young, much like her own voice, and not the deeper voices of the adults. It had an enthusiasm to it.

"Jamie," said Jamie. "Where are you?"

"Over here," said the voice. To Jamie's left, just outside of where she knew the magical barrier was, a soft blue light emerged. The blue light revealed the speaker, a girl who looked to be about the same age as Jamie.

"Who are you?" said Jamie.

"I'm Sam," said the girl. "It's short for Samantha, which some people call me when they get mad at me. That happens to me a lot. I'm a troublemaker."

Jamie looked around at the rest of the room. Everyone else was apparently sound asleep.

"Don't worry about them," said Sam. "They're not going to wake up. They can't hear me anyway. Just you."

"How do you know?" said Jamie.

"I know," said Sam. "It's one of the things I can do."

"So why are you here?" asked Jamie.

"I'm bored," said Sam. "I heard that there were a few visitors captured. It's big news around the village. I heard a rumor that one of them was about my age. It must have been you. So I thought I'd check it out."

"Aren't you going to get in trouble?" asked Jamie.

"Probably," said Sam. "If they catch me. I don't think they're going to catch me. I've gotten pretty good at hiding my tracks."

"Okay," said Jamie.

"Want to get out of here?" said Sam.

"You can do that?" asked Jamie.

"Sort of," said Sam. "A while back they used to put me in these things. Time out, they called it. But I figured a way out of them. Now they have to come up with something else, but they haven't yet."

"So how do I get out of here?" asked Jamie.

"Well, I suppose I should tell you first," said Sam. "I'd get in real trouble if everyone escaped because I let them. I figure they wouldn't notice if you left, as long as I can get you back in here before dawn. You have to promise me that, that you'll come back."

"I can't leave without my mentor and her friends," said Jamie. "I don't know how to sail a boat, even if I had one."

"You don't?" said Sam. "That's easy."

"Well," said Jamie, "I don't live near the ocean, so I never learned."

"Really?" said Sam. "I'm sure there's a lot for you to tell me."

"So how do I get out of here?" asked Jamie.

"Promise you'll come back?" said Sam.

"I promise," said Jamie.

"Okay," said Sam. "I'll tell you how to get out of here. Oh, and don't bother to tell the others how to do it. They won't believe you, or they might try it and it won't work for them, and then they'll just be frustrated. So don't bother."

"All right," said Jamie skeptically.

"Every two minutes and thirteen seconds the shield has to recalibrate its pulses," said Sam. "You can tell it's about to happen because the pulses start to speed up. Once they reset you have seven tenths of a second to jump through the barrier."

"Why would they make it like that?" said Jamie.

"I don't know," said Sam. "I think maybe the person who created the spell got stuck inside one of these one day and had to wait a long time for someone else to figure out how to get her out. So she built in a failsafe. Most traps need one of those."

"Okay," said Jamie. "So when do I go through?"

"You missed one about a minute ago," said Sam. "Just pay attention to the pulses and when they speed up you'll know it's time to go."

"Okay," said Jamie. "Tell me when."

"No," said Sam, "I can't tell you when. If I tell you to jump it'll be too late for you to jump and you'll miss it. You just have to watch yourself. It's coming up soon."

Jamie sensed the magic of the barrier. She could sense it pulsing. She figured it did it about five times per second, but that was accelerating. The pulses increased to a point where it was almost impossible to tell that they were pulsing rather than a steady motion. Then suddenly it all stopped. Jamie crouched and jumped at the barrier. The barrier knocked her back to the ground.

"You missed," said Sam.

"This is going to be hard," said Jamie.

"Don't worry," said Sam, "you were really close that time. You'll get it in a few more tries. It took me five the first time I tried, but that was mostly because I wasn't sure it would work."

"You figured this out on your own?" said Jamie.

"Yeah," said Sam. "Not much else to do when you're in one of these."

Jamie nodded.

It took Jamie three more tries to get it right. When it worked Jamie looked back at the cell, amazed at what she had done.

"I did it," she said.

"Yes," said Sam. "Now let's get out of here."

Jamie and Sam left the prison house. Jamie was surprised to see the dim light of dusk twilight as she left.

"I thought it was nighttime," said Jamie.

"Yeah," said Sam, "those prison rooms do crazy things to your sense of time. They keep everything dark on purpose."

"How long have we been in there?" asked Jamie.

"I don't know," said Sam, "maybe three or four days. I think that's when I first heard about you coming here."

"Four days!" said Jamie. She was suddenly worried about Jay and Dea. What would they do on a desolated beach alone for four days?

"Let's walk down to the beach and watch the stars come out," said Sam.

"Okay," said Jamie. What else could she say?

Along the way they passed a few adults. One of them asked Sam some questions.

"Hello Sam," said the man. "Making trouble again?"

"Trying to stay out of it, Mr. Cheswick," Sam said.

"Who's your new friend?" said Mr. Cheswick.

"Her name's Jamie," said Sam.

"She looks good," said Mr. Cheswick. "Her arms are a little short, but otherwise she looks passable."

"Thanks," said Sam. "I get better every day."

"Run along now," said Mr. Cheswick. "And stay out of trouble."

"Ha," said Sam bitterly, of one who knew that trouble would find her eventually.

"What was that about?" asked Jamie.

"Hm?" said Sam. "Oh, he probably thought you were one of my phantoms."

"Phantoms?" asked Jamie.

"Yeah," said Sam. "There aren't too many girls on the island my age and most of them form a group that's kind of mean, so I try to stay away from them. I sometimes conjure up a phantom to play with."

"You mean like another girl?" asked Jamie.

"Sort of," said Sam. "Don't you ever play pretend?"

"Sometimes," admitted Jamie. She hadn't in a while.

"It helps me talk things through," said Sam, "and sometimes it makes me feel less lonely. Sometimes it doesn't work."

The two had reached the beach. Jamie felt the soft sand beneath her feet as she walked. She liked beaches. She never knew why.

"Here," said Sam. "Let's sit down."

Jamie began to sit down, but Sam pulled her back up.

"Not directly on the sand," said Sam. "Wait."

Sam pointed to the ground. The sand swirled about for a bit, and then up from the sand came two chairs, the backs of which leaned further back than any Jamie had seen before. Sam sat in one. Jamie tapped the chair skeptically, and then sat down.

"How did you do that?" asked Jamie.

"What do you mean?" said Sam.

"The chairs," said Jamie. "Where'd they come from?"

"The sand," said Sam. "Where else would I get them?"

"That's incredible," said Jamie.

"What?" said Sam.

"You can just make chairs?" said Jamie.

"You can't?" said Sam.

"No," said Jamie, as if it were the most preposterous thing in the world.

"Why not?" said Sam. "It's magic."

"I don't have that much magic," said Jamie.

"You don't?" said Sam.

"No," said Jamie. "That's why we're here, I think."

Jamie explained to Sam about the flutterbee, their extinction on the mainland, and the hope of growing a new population on the mainland. She explained about how dragons were the only source of magic, and their power was dwindling.

"So you want to steal some flutterbees?" said Sam.

"We're supposed to take one hive back to Westvalia," said Jamie.

"I don't think we should talk about this anymore," said Sam. "You probably don't know it, but flutterbees are sort of worshipped around here. There are people who make their whole lives out of watching the flutterbees and keeping track of how many there are. Nobody's going to let you touch them."

"I think at this point we'd be happy getting off this island alive," said Jamie.

"No," said Sam, "you could stay here. I'm sure that you could. I don't know about the others but I don't see why you couldn't stay here."

Jamie thought for a second. She didn't give more than a passing thought to the idea of staying on the island, as the notion seemed preposterous to her. She wondered about Sam. What was it that made her want to have Jamie remain on the island in the first place? She thought it might be helpful to have Sam believe that she could stay.

"I don't know," said Jamie, hedging her bets.

"I hope you can," said Sam. "It would be nice to have someone new around. There's never anything new around here."

Jamie looked up at the sky. The stars were coming out.

"Ever wonder about the stars?" asked Sam.

"Sure," said Jamie.

"They're one of the few things magic can't touch," said Sam. "There was one guy in the village a while ago who tried. Crazy Bob, we called him. He swore he would be able to reach out and rearrange the stars in a pattern that resembled his own face."

"What happened?" asked Jamie.

"One morning," said Sam, "someone knocked on the door to his house and there was no answer. They found him in his yard with a large stick pointing skyward. On the ground at the bottom of the stick, the ground was all charred. His feet had been blown off completely, and the shock of it all must have killed him."

"Ouch," said Jamie.

"That was a long time ago," said Sam.

"How long ago?" said Jamie.

"A few hundred years," said Sam. "At least that's how the stories go."

"So you don't really know if that happened at all," said Jamie. "It's just a story you've heard."

"I'm sure it happened," said Sam. "Why would someone lie about that?"

Jamie laughed. "Let me tell you a story," she said.

"Okay," said Sam.

"My mentor's name is Jana," Jamie said. "She's in there trapped with a few other people and I came here with her. Anyway, about a year or so ago she was supposed to be married to the king of Westvalia."

"What's a king?" Sam asked.

"He's the guy who rules over everything," said Jamie. "Don't you have a king?"

"No," said Sam. "We have a council."

"It's probably like that, I guess," said Jamie.

"How can one person be in charge of the entire land?" asked Sam. "I mean, isn't that too much for him to do?"

"I don't know," said Jamie, "he just is. He has an army that works for him, and does what he wants."

"What's an army?" asked Sam.

"An army?" said Jamie. "You don't know what an army is?"

"No," said Sam. "Should I?"

"An army is a big group of soldiers that goes off to war against barbarians," said Jamie, "or protects people from threats."

"You're strange," said Sam.

"Can I get back to my story?" said Jamie.

"Okay," said Sam. "So she was going to marry the king."

"That in itself was a crazy thing," said Jamie, "because Jana and the king had been enemies for about ten years, but that's something I can tell you about later. The king had his reasons for doing what he did, as did Jana. Anyway. Jana's about to get married to the king, and she's walking down the aisle in a grand ballroom, maybe a thousand of Westvalia's most important people there."

"Okay," said Sam.

"Suddenly Sycosina Soulbane shows up," said Jamie. "She's a necromancer, and like Jana was an enemy of the kingdom. She tells Jana that she's going to kill everyone in the room to cleanse Westvalia for its past sins or something. I was there."

"So what happened?" said Sam.

"There was this battle," said Jamie. "Spells were cast everywhere. Sycosina threatened the wedding guests and Jana had to protect them. Eventually Sycosina got the upper hand over Jana, but Jana had a chance at one last fireball. It missed her initially, then circled back to surprise her and hit her. Sycosina fell, and then Jana destroyed her."

"Sounds exciting," said Sam.

"It was," said Jamie. "Jana had saved the kingdom, the king, his brother and sisters, most of the aristocracy, and everyone who was there. She was the hero of the land."

"That's a nice story," said Sam.

"I'm not finished," said Jamie. "In reality, it didn't work out quite like that. Sycosina and Jana had planned the whole thing. Jana figured that her being the hero would put her, and magic, back in the kingdom's good graces. Sycosina figured that her own 'death' would allow her to move freely without the memory of her past deeds—and there were many—hanging over her head. It was a perfect solution for both their problems."

"Okay," said Sam.

"The thing about it is that it will never be remembered like that," said Jamie. "No one will ever tell that the battle had been faked, because it wouldn't be believed. Tybilt—the king—figured it out eventually, but he said that it was in his best interest to cover it up. You see, he didn't really want to marry Jana. He just wanted her on his own side for a fight against the dragons. I don't think he even cared about Sycosina so much."

"So the story wasn't true?" said Sam.

"The story of Jana being the hero is true," said Jamie, "in a way. There are all sorts of other stories I could tell you where the stories don't really match up with the facts. Jana was convinced that the kingdom of Westvalia hated her and hated magic, but in the time leading up to her wedding I found out that most people didn't even know about magic, and barely knew who she was. Jana also told me tales about how the king of Westvalia was a tyrant, but it turned out to not be exactly that way."

"Okay," said Sam.

"And Sycosina Soulbane," said Jamie. "The tales of her are as an evil necromancer, stealing the souls of the righteous for her own use. She had killed hundreds of people in the southwestern plains, but it wasn't because she was a horrid villain doing evil. She was a scared young girl, beset by powers that overwhelmed her and wrought vengeance against the slightest of actions. It was all beyond her control. She never meant to do any of it."

"So?" said Sam. "What's the point?"

"I guess I'm trying to say that you can't just accept a story like that as is," said Jamie. "Anyone who's telling a story may be getting it wrong in the first place, and may be deliberately telling it in such a way to get across some sort of point. I remember being told stories about the Scourge of Wickerton and I know now they were just used to scare me into behaving."

"That's it!" said Sam. "Of course. The story of traveling to the stars fits right into that. It's like anything that has to do with leaving these islands. It's forbidden. I wonder if the story of these islands makes any sense from that perspective."

"Well," said Jamie, "how do they tell it here? I've heard the version from the dragons, but I want to know what you've heard."

"They said that about five thousand years ago," said Sam, "the prophecies foretold total destruction of Vaspen society. They foretold of ancient dragons descending from the sky and reducing our villages to ash and rubble. Our ancestors put their faith in these prophecies, and caused these islands to be split from the mainland. They also weaved a spell to hide the islands from the dragons."

"Our ancestors left behind several orbs of scrying that allowed them to see what had happen. After half a century, the prophecies came true. Dragons descended from the skies and destroyed every village. According to prophecy, the dragons left behind a barren wasteland, devoid of magic, beset by barbarians. We left, never to return."

"But obviously that's wrong," said Sam. "You're here."

"Well," said Jamie, "it fits mostly with what I was told. The thing you missed out on was the taconite. It's a mineral your ancestors supposedly used for a lot of different things that turned out to be toxic to magical creatures. The dragons destroyed your society to save themselves."

"Do you think that's true?" said Sam.

"I have no idea anymore," said Jamie. "I used to trust the dragons, but there's a lot they've done that seems downright sneaky to me. But they said that most of their numbers died while trying to undo the damage of taconite. There are only nine left."

"Only nine?" said Sam. "Three have attacked here over the past few hundred years. The leaders preserved the remains to remind us of the dragons' treachery. I don't know why they were here or what they were doing."

"The thing they told me was that they needed the flutterbees for their young," said Jamie.

"Could be," said Sam. "I know that the council would likely die before allowing the flutterbees to be taken away."

"Even one hive?" said Jamie.

"One hive," said Sam.

"Why?" said Jamie. "There are hundreds of those. If we took one it would probably be replaced within a few months. You wouldn't miss it."

"No," said Sam, "probably not. But I know that's what the council would say."

"Then we're in trouble," said Jamie. "We told them that we were seeking a flutterbee hive."

"Ah," said Sam, "they probably knew that already. One of the benefits of prophecy, I guess."

"So what can I do?" said Jamie. "How do we get out of here?"

"I don't think you need to," said Sam. "You could probably stay here as my friend. I don't think they'd notice if you're gone."

"That's crazy," said Jamie. "I can't stay here."

Sam looked up at the moon. "You need to get back," she said. "Your mentor will notice your absence soon."

"But I don't," said Jamie.

"You will go back now," said Sam, interrupting her. "You won't be able to escape again without my help. If you tell your mentor or anyone else how to escape, they will not believe you."

Jamie shook her head and stared at Sam. She felt like she was going to be her friend, and then suddenly it had turned sour. What was wrong?

"We have to go now."

Sam stood up from the sand and began to walk back toward the village. Jamie followed her with a feeling growing in her gut that there was little point in doing anything else.

They got back to the building where Jana and the others were being held. It looked like an ordinary house, with shingles on the side and a thatched roof. It seemed smaller from the outside than it did on the inside. Sam opened the door and the pair walked in.

"I have to leave you now," said Sam. "I think it was a mistake for me to even come here."

"No, wait," said Jamie. "We can talk about it."

"Goodbye, Jamie," Sam said.

Sam pushed Jamie into the room. Jamie tripped and fell over onto the ground. When she looked back, Sam was gone.

"Wait!" said Jamie.

"Quiet down," said Jana, obviously stirring from sleep.

"Come back!" Jamie yelled again, but again there was no response. She sat down in the middle of the room, frustrated and tired.

Chapter Nine

Discord

"I hate waiting."

Jamie stumbled awake from her sleep to find the adults talking again about whether to try to escape. She worked her way to her feet and thought about what Sam had said.

"Our fate rests in the hand of some isolationists," said Westley. "These are people who left their society five thousand years ago and never saw fit to even try to rejoin it. What chance do you think we have?"

"I don't know," said Jana.

"We need to get out of here," said Westley.

"How?" said Anna. "We've been through this already. This is a prison designed by people who know magic on a far more powerful level than either I or Jana have ever experienced. Don't you think they could design something that would prevent us from breaking out on the inside?"

"It's not like we could just pick a lock," said Mallory.

"That I could do," said Jana.

"I just hate waiting," said Westley. "I hate the idea that there's nothing we could do."

Jamie almost said something at this point, but she was mindful of Sam's warning that the adults would not believe her if she told them. She would have to show them that it was possible first.

As the other four kept arguing, Jamie tried to let their voices recede to the distance. The first thing to do was to listen for the pulses and see if they followed the same pattern as before. They did! Jamie could sense the rhythm speeding up until at one point it reset. She knew she could do this. She just had two minutes and thirteen seconds to wait.

"Jamie, what are you doing?" asked Jana after one minute forty-two seconds.

"Shh," said Jamie, "I'll show you."

Jana waited for a twenty seconds, watching Jamie. The pulses began to speed up.

"Jamie," Jana said, "you know I can tell you're thinking something. You may..."

At the requisite time, Jamie flung herself at the shield. She crashed into the magical barrier and fell back.

"Jamie!" said Jana.

"What do you think you're doing?" asked Anna.

"There's a way out," said Jamie. "I can get out. I know I can. I just need to be able to focus on the timing."

"The timing of what?" said Westley.

"The timing of the pulses," said Jamie.

"How is that supposed to help you?" asked Anna.

"The pulses reset every two minutes and thirteen seconds," said Jamie. "Or something like that. Every time they reset there's a time when you can jump through the barrier. You have maybe half a second to do it but it has to be timed right."

"They reset?" asked Jana.

"Yes," said Jamie. "Wait twenty more seconds and you'll see."

"But..." said Anna.

"Just wait!" said Jamie tersely. The time was coming up and she didn't want to be distracted again.

Jana stuck her hand out at Anna. She was willing to give Jamie another shot.

Jamie felt for the magic again. She could feel the pulses quickening. This was her chance. She felt for the right time, hurled herself at the barrier, and bounced back into the room. So close, and yet not close enough.

"You missed," said Anna matter-of-factly.

"It takes time," said Jamie. "If the timing's not perfect, you, well, you saw."

"Don't beat yourself up, sprite," said Jana.

"I don't think it's worth bothering about," said Anna. "Let's suppose you do get to the other side. What will you do then? Convince the Vaspen to let us out?"

"That's something I can deal with once I'm on the other side," said Jamie.

"Jamie," Jana said, "don't do this. You'll just keep hurting yourself."

"I can do this!" yelled Jamie. "Just let me finish!"

"What makes you think you can?" asked Jana.

"I got out last night," said Jamie. "A Vaspen girl named Sam helped me."

"Oh?" said Anna.

"She said that the prison had a safety mechanism," said Jamie. "Something that would allow the person who crafted the prison spell to get out of the prison if she were trapped inside. It makes sense, don't you think?"

"Maybe," said Anna.

"Hold on," said Jamie. "The time's coming up again."

Jamie felt the pulses growing more rapid. She flung herself at the barrier once again, only to fall back for a third time.

"Are you sure?" asked Jana.

"I got out," said Jamie. "There's a way out, the safety. He had to have built a way out."

"But why put it back in this one?" asked Anna. "Couldn't she just correct it for prisons she has no danger of being put in?"

"There's always a danger," said Jamie. "You could get pushed in. Nobody wants to be trapped in a prison of their own making."

"Jamie," said Jana, "are you sure you just didn't dream the whole thing up?"

"No," said Jamie, "it wasn't a dream."

"You do have a pretty active imagination," said Anna.

"It wasn't a dream," said Jamie. "It was real."

"Sprite," said Jana, "don't beat yourself up. I know you want to help us get out of here, but it's like Anna said. Even if you could get to the other side of the barrier, what would you do? We don't have a boat off this island, and we'll be sure to be caught again. We just have to hope their prophecies tell them to do something other than to kill us."

"No," said Jamie. "It was real. I'll prove it."

Jamie tried again and again to break through the shield. She thought she was close a couple of times, but she never broke through. After sixteen tries in total, she gave up.

"It was real," she said to herself softly.

"I know, sprite," said Jana, "I know. Don't beat yourself up. We all want to get out of here."

Jamie sighed. She could sense that what Sam had showed her was true. The pulses did speed up. There was a gap. But she couldn't find it.

The rest of the day, or what as far as Jamie could tell was a day, was spent in much the same way. Occasionally Westley would make some point about needing to escape, and occasionally Anna would say they needed a plan once they did escape. Despite these obvious needs, no one had yet come up with a way to escape, nor did anyone come up with a plan if they were able to escape. The boat was wrecked beyond repair, and the Vaspen didn't seem to have boats capable of reaching the mainland.

The conversation at one point turned to what the Vaspen council was thinking. The understanding was that there was a small group of Vaspen discussing their fate with regard to some reference to prophecies. The conversation quickly bogged down at that point because there was no way for them to tell what the conversation was like, or how they might influence it in some way.

As the others talked through their suspicions about the council, Jamie lay back against the cold ground and closed her eyes. She tried to imagine what the council was saying.

She saw a group of five Vaspen in a circular white room. Three of the Vaspen were women, and two were men. All but one of them seemed rather old, with their hair greying and their skin wrinkled. The fifth, one of the women, was younger, with long dark brown hair. The five sat around a round table. In the middle of the table was a circular pedestal, and above the pedestal was a flickering image of Jana and Anna.

"There is no doubt, then," one of the older men said. Jamie thought he looked like a Ted, so she named him that.

"These are the red two," said one of the older women, who seemed like an Ellie to Jamie.

"So the prophecies have spoken," said the younger woman, who seemed like a Valerie to Jamie. "The end of our lives is at hand."

"The prophecies are unclear on this point, Valerie," the other old man said. She resolved to call him Robert. "The prophecies tell of an event where the red two appear, but they do not definitely describe an outcome. There are several possibilities."

"Cataclysm is only one possibility," said the last woman, who Jamie decided to call Heather. "We must seek the logical outcome from our actions."

"We should destroy them while we can," said Ted. Jamie took a disliking to Ted.

"I don't think we can be so rash," said Heather. "They may be our salvation as much as they are our doom."

"But what harm can come from it?" said Ted. "If they are gone, it will be as if they had never come."

"But they have come," said Valerie. "Nothing we can do will change that at this point."

"Let us consider why they are here," said Robert. "What did they tell you, Ted?"

"The taller one said that they sought a flutterbee hive," said Ted. "A sacred hive."

"We cannot allow this," said Valerie.

"What if they do succeed?" said Heather. "What do the prophecies say?"

"There are three possibilities," said Robert. "I have foreseen three futures for our people. The actions we take, or fail to take, at this moment, will determine which of these futures will pass. You each know of these prophecies because we have seen them."

"The prophecy of doom," said Ellie, "where our island becomes overrun by tyrannical forces from the mainland."

"The prophecy of desolation," said Ted, "where our island becomes abandoned to the wilds."

"The prophecy of reunion," said Heather, "where our island rejoins the mainland."

"Let us consider," said Robert, "whether these prophecies could come to pass, and which we would like to try to work toward."

"The prophecy of reunion is tempting," said Heather, "but unknowable. It would require reversing the movement of our island, a task that has been tried before and had failed. Those who sent us on our path to begin with took clever assurance that it would be a decision that would be very difficult to reverse. Thrice in our proud history we have tried, and each time we have failed.

"Perhaps then the red ones would help us?" said Robert.

"Impossible," said Valerie. "The prophecies are clear on that point. There will be no cooperation with the red two."

"Can we rule that out?" asked Robert.

The other four looked at each other, and then nodded, some vigorously, while others sadly.

"Sadly," said Heather, "the prophecies are never clear on our own actions. Let us decide this now, though. We must determine a course of action. We must each agree on a course of action. We cannot have dissent on something this important. We must act as one."

"Agreed," said Ted. "We must act with confidence, and as a people."

"There is no surer way to ensure the prophecy of desolation," said Ellie, "than to allow these prophecies to create a division within our society."

"We should destroy them now," said Valerie. "Few know of their existence. It would be as if they had never come."

"But they have come," said Robert. "Nothing we can do will change that now."

Jamie's mind wandered as she started to lose focus on the image of the council. She heard them bickering back and forth, mostly as to Valerie's suggestion that they destroy the visitors. She wanted to close her eyes to think of something else.

She thought of a time long ago, back when she lived on her farm. She was a young girl in her image, no more than seven. She spent some time chasing chickens, hoping to round them up into a corner of the pen for her father to grab. She thought of her times running through the fields of wheat and corn, the plants struggling to grow on a hot summer day. Had she remained there, she almost certainly would have never heard of the Vaspen. But fate dealt her a different hand.

"Psst, wake up!"

The voice caused Jamie to sit up.

"Come on, let's go. I've got a place for you."

It was Sam. Sam was crouched just outside the magical barrier.

"I can't," said Jamie. "I can't get through the barrier."

"Sure you can," said Sam. "Just like last time. I'm here for you."

Jamie shook her head, but there seemed to be no way to convince anyone of anything other than to show them. So Jamie felt for the pulses of the barrier, and waited until they quickened. With little hope, she flung herself at the barrier at what she thought was the right time.

"See," said Sam, "I told you that you could do it."

"What?" said Jamie. "I tried twenty times earlier today to do that and I failed each time."

"You needed me here," said Sam.

"What?" said Jamie. "Why?"

"Because," said Sam. "I said so. Let's go."

Jamie shook her head but then followed Sam. Sam ducked behind a building. She then motioned for Jamie to follow her and sprinted along a dirt path uphill, toward the center of the island.

Jamie followed her, running as she had rarely done before. She found it difficult to keep up with Sam.

"Come on," said Sam. "Hurry."

"Why?" said Jamie.

"I think they know something," said Sam. "I overheard one of the council members talking about you specifically."

"Me?" said Jamie.

"Yeah," said Sam, "which is odd, because the relevant prophecy is the red two. Everyone knows the prophecy of the red two. But we need to watch out."

"Where are we going?" said Jamie.

"Up here," said Sam. "I'll show you."

The pair climbed up the hill for about twenty minutes before Sam cut through the forest. There was no path where she was going, and Jamie was afraid that she wouldn't be able to make it back. Finally they came to a small hill. Sam tugged at some vines to reveal a small door into the side of the hill.

"Let's go," she said.

Jamie followed her through the door and into a small room, no bigger than the shack she had lived in as a child. Sam snapped her fingers and the ceiling of the room began to glow with a soft orange light. In the room was a simple cot and a few books.

"You can stay here," said Sam. "You can stay here until it's safe."

"Thanks," said Jamie. Jamie had so many questions right now but she thought it safer not to ask.

"This is a good hiding spot," said Sam. "They'll never find you here."

"What makes you so sure?" said Jamie.

"It's the way we are," said Sam. "I remember going off to try to hide a few times and it never worked. My parents would find me almost instantly. They would do it even if I had used magic to try to protect myself. Then I realized that the way they can tell where you are hiding is from the magic itself. They don't look for you; they look for the cloak."

"Well," said Sam, "this place is like that. It took me magic to build it, but there's no magic disguising it. Just a bunch of vines and a concealed door. My parents are so used to trying to find me by magic that they've forgotten how to look for things that are hidden by non-magical means."

"Huh," said Jamie.

"So I'm sure you'll be safe here," said Sam.

"That reminds me of something that happened to me," said Jamie. "This was soon after I first met Jana, my mentor. We were following her old apprentice Isabella up a mountain. We couldn't use hardly any magic at all because if we used magic to disguise ourselves, Isabella could see that we were being disguised and confront us right there and then. We had to follow her up to a cave to try to get a pendant."

"What was so important about the pendant?" asked Sam.

"The pendant was the pendant of Solanche," said Jamie. "It was a very powerful magical item that protected the wearer from all forms of physical harm."

"Pff," said Sam, "that's easy."

"Well," said Jamie, "we don't have magic like you do here. There's very little of it."

"So what happened?" asked Sam.

"We got to the cave," said Jamie. "There was a battle between Isabella and the dragon, Kaseraak. Isabella was very clever about using what magic she could to shield some soldiers and keep herself out of harm's way. Eventually Jana outsmarted her."

"Jana?" said Sam.

"That's my mentor," said Jamie. "She's one of the ones with red hair; the taller one."

"Okay," said Sam.

"Anyway, Jana defeated Isabella, and then it came time to face Kaseraak," Jamie said. "But there was no need for a further fight. Kaseraak was friendly, and somewhat grateful to Jana for saving him from Isabella. He gave Jana the pendant."

"So it all worked out, then?" said Sam.

"Yes," said Jamie. "Then Jana destroyed the pendant."

"What?" said Sam. "Why?"

"She said it wouldn't protect her from the things she needed protection from," Jamie said, "and that it was too great a risk that someone else would get it."

"That's strange," said Sam.

"I thought so at the time," said Jamie, "but I understand why she did it."

"That sounds like quite an adventure," said Sam.

"I've had a few," said Jamie.

"I wish I could have adventures," said Sam. "The biggest adventures for me so far are running away from my house. Generally I return within a few hours because there's nothing else to do. It's not like I can go to another village or anything."

"You have some amazing things here," said Jamie.

"So there's no magic where you are?" said Sam.

"Well, there's some," said Jamie. "Jana's teaching me how to use it. But it's not like it is here. I mean, there's not enough magic at home for me to fly."

"I wonder what it's like," said Sam.

"It's boring," said Jamie.

"I mean," said Sam, "how do you make a house?"

Jamie blinked. That wasn't something she had thought about before.

"Well," said Jamie, "you get some wood, dig a hole in the ground, and make a frame, I guess…"

"You do it all manually?" said Sam.

"Manually?" said Jamie.

"Yeah," said Sam, "that's what we call it when we make something without magic here."

"Yeah," said Jamie.

"That must take a while," said Sam.

"It does," said Jamie.

"Here," said Sam. "I want to show you something."

"Okay," said Jamie.

Sam formed a ball with her hand. Her hands began to sparkle. Jamie saw strands of light shoot out from between Sam's fingers. She looked on with curiosity. About half a minute later, Sam opened her hands to reveal a butterfly.

It was the most beautiful butterfly Jamie had ever seen. Its wings were a bright orange with a large black stripe and a small white stripe surrounding its frame. Within the black stripes were yellow dots that seemed to sparkle with light from an unknown source. Jamie watched the butterfly as it flitted about the room.

"We can do almost anything magic," said Sam. "My father once told me that we were limited only by our imaginations."

"So if you can imagine it," said Jamie, "you can do it."

"For the most part," said Sam. "I mean, that butterfly will disappear into nothingness once I've stopped thinking about it. But basically, it doesn't take all that much training. I mean, nobody taught me how to do that. I just figured it out."

"Is everyone here like that?" said Jamie.

"Sort of," said Sam. "I think most kids go through a time where they're creating butterflies or flutterbees or toy bears or whatever. I don't think everyone does what I do though."

"What do you do?" said Jamie. "You mean imagine friends for yourself?"

"Yeah," said Sam.

"Why do you do that?" said Jamie.

"Nobody understands me," said Sam. "Everyone just goes along with the prophecies and trusting in the wisdom of the council and everything, and nobody ever thinks to wonder whether it might all be wrong. I mean, I've seen what some of the adults can do. They can dig wells down hundreds of feet and create pumps that irrigate crops evenly, all in a couple days time. The whole island could be changed by that. We can do anything we want and we choose to remain on an island in the middle of nowhere because of some prophecy? What sense does that make?"

"The prophecy of reunion?" asked Jamie.

"Something like that," said Sam. She looked at Jamie and cocked her head to the side. "How do you know about that?"

"You must have said something about it," said Jamie.

"I don't think so," said Sam.

"Well, maybe someone else did," said Jamie. "What are prophecies, anyway? We don't believe in any such things."

"They are visions of the future," said Sam. "Apparently the ones on the council are the people who can view the prophecies and divine their meaning. Not all are so grand. Sometimes we have a prophecy of rain, and it will rain two days later. The little things come true and give us reason to have faith in the larger prophecies. I think the council spends most of their days searching into the big prophecies in order to best prepare for them."

"So what are the big prophecies?" asked Jamie.

"Well," said Sam, "the one that everyone knows about is the prophecy of the red two. The big problem with that, unlike a lot of other prophecies, is that no one knows how that will turn out."

"What do you mean?" said Jamie.

"We're told to believe in the power of prophecy," said Sam. "It's what allowed us to survive all those years ago, and it prepared us for the attack of the dragons. Of course, none of this was actually in my lifetime, or even close. But these are the legends people tell. In class I get drilled on the details of the history. We have quizzes."

"Class?" said Jamie.

"Yeah," said Sam. "Six days a week. Usually I cut at least one of those days, but too much more and I get thrown into time out."

"What's class?" said Jamie.

"You don't have classes?" said Sam.

"No, well, I guess," said Jamie. "It's been a long time. Not since I became Jana's apprentice. She just teaches me when she can, mostly through following her around and learning. But when I was growing up in a little village on the farm I did have a couple classes, I guess. A couple hours a week."

"A couple hours a week?" said Sam. "Can I go there? What else did you do the whole time?"

"I worked on the farm," said Jamie.

"What do you mean?" said Sam. "Farming is so boring."

"Well," said Jamie, "mostly I went around pulling out weeds. Sometimes I got to feed the chickens or collect eggs."

"You did it yourself?" said Sam.

"Yeah," said Jamie.

"We don't have any weeds here," said Sam. "We don't touch the plants. Why don't you do it that way?"

"We don't have magic," said Jamie. "Not that much of it, anyway. Only a few people know how to use it."

"That seems so strange to me," said Sam. "What's it like?"

"Well," said Jamie, "it's normal, I guess."

"Do you even have houses?" said Sam. "How can you do that much physical work?"

"You just do," said Jamie. "We have big cities."

"What's it like there?" said Sam. "Tell me about the city."

"Well," said Jamie, "the capital city is called Westvalia. It's located at the junction of a couple rivers just upstream from a bay along the western sea. There's a large palace in the center where the king lives. In the center of the city is a large library, which holds all the books and scrolls and stories that people have written over the years. I should see if there's anything about the Vaspen, or the dragons, but I think that's so long ago there might not be anything there."

"So tell me about the city," said Sam. "How many people live there?"

"I'm told that there are a couple hundred thousand people," said Jamie, "though that probably includes the tent cities."

"A couple hundred thousand?" said Sam. "That's crazy. There are only a hundred eighty of us on this island, just over five hundred in total. I can see why the prophecy of doom has taken hold."

"The prophecy of doom?" said Jamie. She remembered it from her dream or imagination, but she was surprised to hear it confirmed.

"That's one of the three futures," said Sam. "Everyone knows the three futures. We have that drilled into our heads."

"So how can you have three futures?" asked Jamie. "I mean, isn't the point of prophecy that it tells the future?"

"I asked that question a while ago," said Sam. "What they told me is that prophecies are possibilities, not certainties. Sometimes one vision will hold true because it's more likely than the others. Prophecies aren't set in stone. The original prophecies that sent us away from the mainland were that we would go extinct. Obviously that didn't happen because we did something about it. The prophecy of the dragon attack was originally thought to destroy our village, but we lived through that."

"So what happens in the prophecy of the red two?" said Jamie.

"That's the odd thing about it," said Sam. "It's not like a normal prophecy with a set result, like learning it will rain. The advanced seers have identified it as a point—an inflection point if I remember it right—something that affects the rest of our destiny. And it's not hard to see why."

"Why?" asked Jamie.

"It's the first visit from the mainland," said Sam. "The first proof that there are actual people still there. For the prophecy of reunion it gives us a reason to go back there. For the prophecy of doom it provides an enemy who will come down to destroy us. The prophecy of desolation is a bit trickier but I think it has to do with too many people leaving the island. The common understanding of the prophecy of the red two is that our response to it will determine which of the other three prophecies will happen."

"But that's ridiculous," said Jamie. "It's ridiculous to think that one point in time can forever alter your future."

"That's not our way," said Sam. "Some of the elders like to run traces back in time and they can attribute major differences in an individual's life by an innocent choice taken long ago."

"We need to get out of here," said Jamie.

"No," said Sam. "You can't leave like that. They'll stop you, or maybe even kill you trying to escape."

"But they'll know I'm gone," said Jamie. "They'll be out searching for me and by me escaping it will have made things worse."

"Trust me on this," said Sam. "Please, just trust me. Everything will be okay."

"No it won't be okay!" said Jamie. "They're going to kill Jana, and Anna, and Westley, and Mallory, and if I don't do anything it will be my fault."

"Please," said Sam. "Stay here. You'll be okay."

Jamie fumed.

"Look," said Sam, "I've got to go. Otherwise they'll notice I'm gone. You'll be safe here, I promise. Just stay here."

"Okay," said Jamie.

"Promise?" said Sam.

"I promise," said Jamie.

Sam left through the door. Jamie walked over to the door and checked it. The seal was tight, but the door wasn't locked. She could leave if she wanted to.

Jamie thought about her promise to Sam. She thought about the danger to Jana and the rest of the crew. She sat back and tried to imagine what things would be like when it was discovered that she was gone.

Jana would be worried. What would she think? Jamie figured that Jana wouldn't believe that she had escaped somehow. She thought that maybe they would think that she was taken. If only Jamie could get a message to Jana that she was okay.

She thought back to something Sam had said, and something that she had seen earlier. A while back, she had learned of a spell called a familiar. The idea was that someone could create a magical object resembling an animal, and then use the animal's eyes to see what was going on there. The ancient dragon Norzakind had used a very complicated version of the spell to spy on the kingdom of Westvalia. Norzakind's version of the spell created an avatar that for most purposes was human; only mages could see through the spell and know that it was something else.

Jamie decided that she didn't need something all that fancy. A small mouse would work. But how could she craft a mouse? Where would she begin? She wished she had someone to tell her how to do it, but this was something that Jana herself didn't know how to do. Jamie wondered if the magic around her could make it possible anyway.

For the first hour, Jamie started simply. She tried to create something that looked like a mouse from the magical energy that surrounded her. Jamie had seen hundreds of mice before. Sometimes they were serious problems, back on her farm. Sometimes they were the food for a cat. Jamie gathered magical energy together and tried to make it into some form. After a minute, she found that she could create a small wooden block. After a half hour's worth of work, the block resembled an animal of some sort. After a full hour and a half, Jamie had created something that looked kind of like a mouse. It would have to do. Jamie was exhausted.

The next problem Jamie had to tackle was getting control over the mouse. She thought about how she would often drift off to sleep and imagine how things were elsewhere. She thought about how she had seen the meeting of the Vaspen council. Inspiration struck her: she had actually learned the real three future prophecies of the Vaspen. What Sam said lined up with what Jamie had imagined, and Jamie had imagined it first. She must have actually seen a council meeting.

Long ago, Jamie had met a mage named Talia. Talia's speciality was called divination, if Jamie remembered the word properly. Talia could take an object and see remnants of its past. Jamie felt that she was discovering something similar. She had no idea how Talia did it, as Talia was not the friendliest of mages. But she knew it could be done.

Jamie started first by creating the mouse. Then she tried to drift off into her imagination, as she had done previously. Unfortunately for Jamie, this meant that she lost her concentration on the mouse and it disappeared as soon as she stopped thinking about it. In order for the spell to work, Jamie had to concentrate on two things at once. Jana had never taught her how to do that. Jamie spent another two hours frustrated, unable to hold the two spells at once.

After two hours, Jamie had another inspiration. In her previous attempts, she had created the mouse and then tried to put her mind into it. She suddenly realized that she might have gotten in backwards. What would happen if she drifted off into her imagination, and then tried to build a mouse around it? She tried that and was so surprised to find that it had succeeded for a second that she lost concentration and found herself snapped back to her body. But now that she knew how to do it, it was just a matter of time.

Jamie spent the next two hours practicing the spell. Initially, she couldn't hold it for more than a few seconds. After some practice, she could hold it for minutes at a time. When she was able to run around the room with the mouse for a little under half an hour, she was confident that she could hold it as long as necessary.

Jamie took a short break to consider what to do next. She felt like she needed to get some word to Jana that she was okay, but how would she do that? Could she use the mouse to scratch out a message? After a few moments trying, she gave up on that idea. The mouse's paws were too weak to write anything in the hard dirt floor. Getting there would have to be enough.

Jamie cast the spell and found herself in the mouse's body. She scurried underneath the door and out to the forest. At that point she realized a flaw in her plan. She had no idea how to get back to the village, as there was no path and her view as a mouse was obstructed by bushes and roots and even small piles of dirt. She looked to the sky. It was nighttime, and she remembered that she would need to head west to get to the village. After a few moments, she scurried down a hill, hoping that she was going in the right direction. About twenty minutes later, she had reached a field, but the grass was too tall for her to see over. She searched the field for a rock, but could not find one.

Eventually she came to a cultivated plot. The plot had neat rows of corn, stretching for a couple hundred yards in one direction. Along the edges of the plot were stone walls, each about two feet tall. Jamie was able to crawl onto one of them, and from the wall she was able to spot the village. From there it was a simple matter of running along paths toward the village. In total it took Jamie an hour and a half to find the village.

Jamie relaxed for a split second. She had been holding the spell for far longer than she had ever concentrated on any spell. In a brief panic, she felt her concentration slipping. She snapped back into focus, maintaining the spell. She couldn't relax now, she resolved. It took her five more minutes to find the house holding her friends.

She squeezed under the door and looked to the prison. She couldn't tell it, but she knew that there was a barrier in the room she couldn't pass. If she had gotten close to the magical barrier holding the group inside, her spell would break instantly. She kept her distance along the far wall.

Jana was pacing back and forth. The other three were seated, their backs against the far wall of the room.

"Where is she?" said Jana. "Why did they take her?"

"You can ask us as many times as you like," said Westley. "We still don't have the answers."

Jamie made the mouse squeak. It was far too soft a sound for anyone to hear at that distance.

"What monsters are they?" said Jana. "She's just a kid."

"She's thirteen," said Anna.

"So?" said Jana.

"Give her a little credit," said Anna, "that's all. When you were thirteen you wanted to take on the world."

Nobody said anything more for a minute. Jamie thought of a plan. Could she walk up to the barrier? She wanted Jana to know that she was safe, but how could she know that from a mouse?

A moment later, the door opened. Two people walked in. Jamie recognized them from her vision as Ted and Valerie, the two least friendly Vaspen on the council.

"What have you done with her?" yelled Jana as they entered.

Jamie cowered in the corner, partly in fright from the strength of Jana's voice, and partly to hide from the Vaspen.

Ted and Valerie looked at Jana for a moment. They then looked about the room. Ted nodded slowly.

"That is not your concern, Jana Aliston," Ted said.

"She's my apprentice so it damn well is my concern," said Jana.

Valerie turned to Ted and ignored Jana's comment. "It is as you say," she said.

"Answer me!" Jana said.

"You are in no position to make demands," said Valerie.

"Where is she?" asked Anna in a voice slightly less angry than Jana's.

"She is safe," said Valerie. "She is being questioned."

Jamie may have squeaked softly. Luckily for her, no one noticed.

"Why her?" said Jana. "She doesn't know anything."

"Do you know something?" asked Ted.

"We've told you everything that we can tell you," said Jana.

"How many dragons are left alive?" said Valerie.

"What?" said Jana.

"You heard me," Valerie said tersely. "How many dragons are left alive?"

"I don't know for certain," Jana said.

"Rumor has it at around ten," said Anna.

"We fought the dragons off once before," said Ted. "We can do it again."

"I saw," said Jana. "I'm sure you can."

"You are working for them," said Ted, "admit it."

"I told you before," said Jana, "I'm doing this for me. The dragons suggested it but I don't serve them."

"Why do you take us for fools?" said Valerie. "We can read your thoughts. We know that you do the dragons' bidding."

"I don't," said Anna.

"It doesn't matter," said Ted. "We've heard all that we need to hear. This should be enough to convince the council."

"Convince the council of what?" said Jana.

"That our best course is to destroy you," said Valerie. "You are the sign of a larger invasion, and should we permit you to return to the mainland our island will be overrun with your barbaric forces."

"You must be joking," said Jana. "What would we want with this piddly island?"

"I don't joke," said Valerie.

"Goodbye, red two," said Ted. "The next time we meet will be your last."

The two Vaspen left the room. Jana began pacing again.

"What do we do now?" said Anna.

Jana cursed under her breath.

"Jana!" said Anna.

"I don't know," said Jana. "There's nothing we can do about this prison. We can't get out. Jamie's out there somewhere being grilled. Who knows what she's told them?"

"Would it make a difference?" said Anna.

"No," said Jana, "probably not. They'll believe what they want to believe. Stupid prophecies."

"Well," said Mallory, "it's not exactly unsurprising. Living isolated like this for five thousand years has got to do funny things to their brains."

"I wish the dragons would have told me," said Jana. "I wish they would have been honest. I might have been better prepared."

"Do you really think that would have mattered?" said Anna.

"I don't know," said Jana. "Right now I'm just worried about Jamie. She shouldn't have to go through something like this."

Jamie inched her way toward Jana. She didn't want to touch the barrier, but she wanted to get her attention somehow.

"We need to get out," said Anna.

"There's no way," said Jana. "Our magic just isn't powerful enough."

Jana ran at the barrier and crashed against it with her body. The force of the magic knocked her back, sending her tumbling into Westley.

"Watch it," said Westley.

"Jana!" said Anna. "What are you doing?"

"Trying to get out of here," said Jana. "I'm just frustrated."

"That's not the way to do it," said Anna.

Jamie squeaked loudly. That was exactly the way to do it.

"I know," said Jana. "I'm just frustrated."

Jamie ran up in the middle of the room. She was more confident, as she knew where the barrier was now. She squeaked as loudly as she could.

"What's that?" asked Mallory. She pointed at Jamie.

"It's a mouse," said Anna.

Jamie squeaked.

"That's the funniest looking mouse I've ever seen," said Mallory.

Jamie began squeaking and scratching at the floor.

"What's it doing?" said Anna. "Don't mice usually stay hidden?"

"What do we care?" said Westley. "It's just a stupid mouse."

Jamie squeaked again.

"Shoo, mouse," Anna said.

Jamie shook her head. With one paw she tried to point at Jana.

"Shoo," said Anna.

"Leave the mouse alone," said Jana. "It's just a stupid mouse."

Jana began pacing. Jamie followed her from side to side.

"The mouse is following you," said Mallory.

"What?" said Jana.

Jamie squeaked as Jana knelt down at the barrier to look at her closer. Jamie started jumping up and down.

"What does it want?" said Anna.

"It's a mouse," said Jana. "It probably wants some cheese."

Jamie tried rolling over on her back and from side to side. Her frustration was beginning to affect her focus.

Mallory walked over toward Jana and knelt beside her to look at Jamie.

"That's not a mouse," said Mallory.

Jamie squeaked and pointed at Mallory.

"What?" said Jana.

"What is it?" said Anna.

"I don't know," said Mallory. "But mice don't have tails that long, and don't have feet that short, and the fur is all wrong. The eyes are the wrong color, too."

Jamie squeaked loudly and pointed at Mallory.

"But if it's not a mouse," said Westley, "what is it?"

Jana looked at the mouse and turned her head to the side. "Jamie?"

Jamie squeaked loudly and jumped up.

"What?" said Anna.

"You think that's Jamie?" asked Mallory.

Jamie ran quick circles, trying to express excitement.

"Jamie," said Jana, "if that's you, stand up on your hind legs."

Jamie stood up on her hind legs. It took a lot of effort for her to do so. She fell back down after a half a second.

"It is her!" said Anna.

"Jamie," said Jana, "I don't know where you are, but believe me, we'll figure a way out of this. We'll find you."

Jamie squeaked and did her best to look disappointed.

"How is she doing that?" asked Mallory.

"I don't know," said Jana. "But she's pretty creative."

Jamie squeaked.

"We'll find you, Jamie," said Jana. "We'll get you out of here."

Jamie squeaked again. She circled around and scratched at the floor.

"How?" said Anna.

"I don't know," said Jana.

Jamie squeaked. She would just have to show them how. She tried to sense the barrier, and was dimly aware of the pulses. It was almost too much for her to handle, to control the motion of a mouse, see through it, and sense magical energy. For a brief ten seconds she could do it. She felt the pulses quicken, and realized she had one shot at this. She ran back, leapt at the magical barrier, and hoped it worked.

Chapter Ten

Escape

"Jamie, wake up!"

Jamie shook her head slowly. A moment later she felt something slapping her cheeks softly.

"Wake up!"

Jamie lifted her hand to block the hand from slapping her cheeks. She opened her eyes slowly.

"Oh good," Sam said. "You're awake."

"I what?" said Jamie. She shook her head. She felt very dizzy.

"You're awake," said Sam. "When I got here you were out cold. I was worried."

"How long was I asleep?" said Jamie.

"I don't know," said Sam. "It's been maybe twenty hours since I left you here."

"Twenty hours!" said Jamie.

"What were you doing?" said Sam.

"I was just trying out some new spells," said Jamie.

"You can't," said Sam. "If they sense the magic here, they might find you. You have to stay here."

"And do what?" said Jamie. "Stay here forever?"

"No," said Sam, "just until it's safe."

"When will it be safe?" said Jamie.

"I don't know," said Sam.

"When Jana and Anna are dead?" said Jamie.

"I don't know," said Sam.

"They're going to kill them," said Jamie. "They said they would. I saw them. I need to help them."

"You can't help them," said Sam.

"They know I'm gone," said Jamie. "Something's going to happen to them, and it's because I left. You said so yourself."

"What?" said Sam.

"Don't you see?" said Jamie. "Because I escaped they think that it's a sign of the prophecy of doom. They think that unless they can kill us all, the prophecy of doom will come true. They think we're set on getting the dragons the power they need to come here and finish off this island."

"No," said Sam.

"Yes, it is," said Jamie. "My friends are going to die unless I can figure out something to do about it."

"No," said Sam, "you'll be fine here. Just stay here, everything will be fine. I'll handle it."

"You'll handle it?" said Jamie. "You're just a kid like me. How can you convince anyone of anything?"

"I don't know," said Sam.

"I need to go help Jana," said Jamie. "I know how to get them out. I've got to do this."

"Please don't," said Sam. "It's very dangerous now, but if you can wait a while…"

"Wait a while?" said Jamie, interrupting Sam. "Wait for what? I'm a human, here on this Vaspen island, an intruder to your way of life. People think I'm a sign of the prophecy of doom. There's no way I'm going to ever be safe on this island. What in the world makes you think I will be?"

Sam stood quietly by Jamie. She looked down at the ground.

"Well?" said Jamie.

Sam leapt forward and embraced Jamie in a hug.

"Just be my friend," said Sam.

Jamie blinked and looked around.

"I'm so lonely," said Sam. "No one, none of them understands. There's no one here who understands me."

Jamie blinked again. She wrapped her hands around Sam's back and patted her gently.

"You're the only one who understands me," Sam said. "You're the only one that knows how much I want to get out of this place, and how hard it is to live on an island with nothing more to hope for that just living on the island. I want to do something, I want to go somewhere, but whenever I say anything it's dismissed as silly or impossible. You don't do that. You know."

"I don't know," said Jamie. She was struggling for the words to say. She did feel some sort of kinship with Sam; four years ago, after all, Jamie was trapped on a farm with no reasonable chance of moving to something better, not until Jana came along. Could Jamie be Sam's hope, as Jana was to Jamie? She wondered about that for a second.

"I know your friends are in trouble," said Sam. "I can't do anything about that. I'd get in real trouble if I did."

"Maybe you will," said Jamie, "maybe you won't."

"Could you take me with you?" said Sam.

"I don't know," said Jamie. "Are you sure you'd want to?"

"I've been dreaming for years of getting off this island," said Sam.

"What about your parents?" said Jamie.

"They don't care," said Sam.

"We'll see," said Jamie. "First I need to figure out how to get my friends out."

"They won't believe you if you tell them how to escape as you did," said Sam. "You'll have to find another way."

"I have an idea," said Jamie.

Jamie wrapped herself in dark clothes and a hood. She had imagined the clothes and that, apparently, was sufficient to actually create them. They weren't fashionable, but they would hide her from plain sight. She thought about trying to figure out the disguise spells

Anna and Jana had used to sneak through Westvalian camps in the past, but she decided against it. Magic would, by itself, draw attention to her, and she didn't want that. She had to trust the darkness of her new clothes. Her hopes were heightened by Sam's advice that the Vaspen were particularly bad at spotting non-magical disguises.

Jamie left the hiding spot and stumbled through the forest back toward the path. It was late at night now, and the full moon hung over the southern sky, providing enough light for Jamie to see, but hopefully not enough for her to be seen. A half hour or so later, Jamie reached the village.

The village was dark this time of night. No one was out on the streets. Jamie made her way through the dirt streets back to where the cell was. She reflected that the Vaspen had apparently put so much faith on their magic that they hadn't bothered to guard their prisoners. She also thought that they might have had insufficient numbers in the entire little village to assign that duty to someone.

Jamie opened the door and ducked inside. Jana and the rest of the crew were resting, if not sleeping, and hadn't noticed her arrival. Jamie walked up to the magical barrier and crouched down to whisper to Jana.

"Jana!" said Jamie in the loudest whisper she could muster.

Jana stirred. She looked directly at Jamie. She then looked around the room and then back at Jamie.

"Jamie!" Jana said. "Are you okay? Did they hurt you?"

"I'm fine," said Jamie. "I escaped."

"Yeah," said Jana, "we saw your mouse. How did you get away from them?"

"They didn't take me anywhere," said Jamie. "I broke out of the prison and they haven't found me. We need to get everyone out of here."

"But how?" said Jana.

Anna, Westley and Mallory were awake by this time. They kept crouched low to the ground, as if there were something about the ceiling they wanted to avoid.

"It's like I told you earlier," said Jamie. "Every two minutes or so, the shield resets, and there's a gap of about half a second when you can jump through. You have to time it exactly right."

"Sprite," said Jana, "we went through that. You tried it. It didn't work."

"It did work," said Jamie. "That's how I'm out here."

"There has to be something more to it," said Jana, "something that you did differently but you just didn't know about it."

"There's nothing more to it than that," said Jamie. "The time's coming up in ten seconds. Get ready to jump."

"Okay, sprite, but," said Jana.

"Jump now!" said Jamie.

Jana jumped forward and was slammed back by the magical barrier into her sister.

"Ow," said Anna.

"You were too late," said Jamie.

"It's not going to work," said Jana.

"I'm never going to convince you of this," Jamie said, muttering under her breath. She looked up, realizing that she had just echoed something Sam had said to her.

"What?" said Jana.

"You're right," said Jamie. "This is precisely how not to escape."

"What?" said Anna.

"You shouldn't sense the vibrations of the shield," said Jamie. "They always remain steady, and certainly don't increase in pace. And by no means will they ever reset."

Jana cocked her head to the side and looked at Jamie.

"They will never give you a chance to escape," said Jamie, "not even for half a second."

"Okay, Jamie," Jana said. "I think I see what you're saying."

"Don't even try," said Jamie. "It will be pointless and you will just hurt yourself."

Jana nodded slowly.

"This prison is unbreakable," said Jamie. "It's the most advanced spell designed by Vaspen, and they certainly wouldn't leave a way out a thirteen year old girl could discover."

Jana braced herself. She could sense the pulses of the shield quickening.

"Ready," Jana said.

"You don't have ten seconds," said Jamie.

Ten seconds passed. Anna, Westley and Mallory watched on with anticipation. Jana crouched and took a flying leap at the barrier. A split second later, she tumbled to a landing on the other side.

"You made it!" Jamie said.

"So I did," said Jana.

"Now what?" asked Anna. "I might be able to do the same thing, but without being able to detect magic, Westley and Mallory would have no chance at it."

"Let's see," said Jana. "I was able to create a small hole in the barrier from the inside using just my gems. Now that I'm outside I might be able to create a larger opening."

"Get to it," said Westley. "They could return at any time."

Jana closed her eyes and began to focus. Jamie could sense that she was fighting hard against the barrier. She saw a hole open up in the barrier along the ground. It was about two and a half feet round.

"Get out," said Jana. "Now."

Anna crawled toward the barrier. She managed to get through without incident. She stood up next to Jamie.

"Where is it?" said Mallory. "Do we follow where Anna went?"

"Here," said Jamie, "I think I can show you."

Jamie focused her mind on the barrier. She imagined the swirling energies and then imagined them glowing a deep red. When she opened her eyes she could see the barrier glowing, with a hole ready for Mallory and Westley to crawl through.

"Thanks, sprite," Westley said.

Jamie smiled.

"Where do we go now?" said Jana.

"I've got a place where we can hide," said Jamie.

Jamie led the group out of the building and then up into the forest. Forty minutes later, they found the hideout. It was rather cramped with five people, but it was a place where they could stay.

"How did you find this?" Anna asked.

"A friend showed me," said Jamie. "She said that they rely almost exclusively on magical ways of hiding yourself and finding hidden things, so much that they overlook things that are hidden normally. That's how I got into town."

"Good job, sprite," said Jana. "Good job."

Jamie smiled.

"Now what?" said Anna. "We may be out of the village but they must realize at some point that we're gone and they'll start looking for us. We may be hidden well, but eventually they'll find us again."

"And they might decide then that they shouldn't give us a second chance to escape," said Westley.

"The sun's going to come up soon," said Mallory.

"Yeah," said Jana. "I think we need to wait until the sun sets again. It will be easier to move in the dark."

"Move where, though?" said Westley.

"Back to the ship," said Jana. "We need to get out of here."

"The ship's wrecked," said Westley. "What's the point in getting there?"

"We'll figure something out," said Jamie.

The group spent the day resting. Jamie had interrupted the rest from the night before, so they needed it to be alert for their planned escape.

In the midmorning, Jamie felt her first magical scan. It felt like a wave of magical energy passing over her. She had gotten used to detecting changes in magical energy so this one was hard for her to miss. It was an intense wave of magical energy passing through her, from one side of the room to the other.

"What was that?" said Jamie.

"Was what?" said Westley.

"You felt it too?" said Anna.

Jamie nodded.

"My guess is that it's how they're trying to find us," said Jana. "They're sending out waves of energy and seeing what happens when they come back. Any change in the returned energy will mean a use of magic somewhere."

"That makes sense," said Anna, "as long as they think we're using magic somehow."

"I told you," said Jamie. "We can stay hidden here and they won't be able to find us."

"We can't stay hidden forever," said Mallory.

"No," said Jana. "We'll wait for tonight."

Over the course of the day the waves of magical energy passed through the group, generally once every ten to twenty minutes. Sometimes the wave was strong. Sometimes the wave was weaker.

"Unless they're varying the intensity deliberately," said Jana, "I bet that's a sign of how close they are to us."

Anna and Jamie nodded.

"I still have no idea what you're talking about," said Westley.

Jamie opened her mouth to try to explain, but Jana motioned for her to stop.

"It's magic stuff," said Jana. "You wouldn't understand."

Westley shrugged and the group let it be.

The group didn't get much rest over the day. There wasn't much else for the group to do, but the presence of the magical waves was unnerving. At any moment someone could appear and find them and no one could imagine a credible defense. Having escaped once, they were worried that the next time they were captured, they would be killed rather than imprisoned. Jana and Westley felt certain of that.

The evening fell and the room got darker. Up until that point, there was no sign that the Vaspen had any idea where they were. Jana and Westley began discussing a plan for the group. During the night, they would slip out and make their way toward the ship. Once they got to the ship, they would evaluate the situation there. There was no talk about the flutterbees. At this point, the group was focused on escape and survival.

Sometime during the discussion Jamie heard a rustling of the leaves outside. Jamie held up her hand for the group to be quiet. At first they couldn't tell if it was anything other than the wind. After a few seconds, they heard it again. Someone was around outside.

"What do we do?" whispered Jamie.

Jana put her finger to her mouth to motion to Jamie to be quiet. At that very moment, Jamie felt a wave of magical energy pass through her. Another sweep, she thought, this one strong. Jamie felt her muscles tighten up. She heard the sound of vines scraping against the door.

Then she heard a knock on the door.

Nobody moved.

Whoever it was knocked again.

"Jamie!" came a loud whisper from outside.

"Open the door," said Jamie, "it's okay."

Nobody moved. Jamie broke free from her self-induced paralysis and moved to open the door. Sam pushed through the opening and stepped inside, closing the door quickly behind her.

"Sam," said Jamie.

"I hoped you would be here," said Sam. "I hoped you hadn't left already."

Sam sat a bag down on the ground in front of her.

"What's that?" said Jamie.

"It's my stuff," said Sam. "I want to come with you."

"No," said Jamie.

"Who are you now?" said Jana.

"Oh," said Jamie, "this is Sam. She's the one who helped me escape. She made this hideout for me."

Jamie went around the room and introduced Sam to everyone. After they had all swapped names, Jana took charge of the conversation.

"We can't take you with us," said Jana.

"I don't have anything here," said Sam.

"You don't have any family here?" said Jana.

"Well, there's my mom and my dad," said Sam, "and my little brother. But they all hate me."

"We can't take you away from your parents," said Anna.

"Look," said Sam, "if I stay here, what's going to happen to me? I'll be stuck on this island all my life, just like every other person I know. I don't want that. I want adventure. I want to see the world."

"It's a dangerous place," said Jana.

"Look," said Sam, "I'm thirteen. I'm old enough to decide for myself where to go now. And I want to go with you."

"How can you know that?" said Anna. "You know nothing about what life is like where we are. You've lived a cushy life here with magic allowing you to do almost anything. You wouldn't even know anyone."

"I'd know one person," said Sam.

"You know," said Westley, "I was thirteen when I went on my first boat sailing around the southern coast to Westvalia. I understand the allure of adventure. But then I knew I could always come back. No one comes back here. You'd be gone for good."

"I don't care," said Sam. "You said what it was like. Where were you when you were thirteen?"

"I was apprenticing with Lady Vissara," said Jana. "We traveled the lands, in what I know now to be allies in her attempt to overthrow the king."

"I was apprenticing with Karsha," said Anna. "We weren't about to take over the world, but I was learning to be a mage in my own right."

"I was off in the woods," said Mallory, "hunting and foraging for food for my family. I could take care of myself."

"See?" said Sam. "You all at age thirteen were well on your way to being free and making your own decisions. You two," she said while pointing to Jana and Westley, "were traveling the lands. Is it so wrong for me to want to do that?"

"It's one thing to do it and know you can come back home," said Jana. "It's another thing to leave forever."

"I don't care," said Sam. "Do you want my help or not?"

"I want your help," said Jamie.

"We want your help," said Jana. "It's just that we're not sure it's right for you."

"Plus the Vaspen might be ruthless to us if they thought we were kidnapping one of their children."

"Don't worry," said Sam. "They won't. I've written a note."

"A note?" asked Jana.

"I told them I was leaving," said Sam.

"Great," said Anna. "Now they're sure to think we're taking you."

"Look," said Sam, "you don't have much time. We need to go soon or else everyone will be on top of us. They may take some time to find this place but they'll find it eventually. You can either take my help or not."

"Well," said Jana, her voice drifting off in thought.

"You're going to have trouble getting off this island without me," said Sam. "You need me."

"She's right," said Jamie.

"Okay," said Jana. "I don't like it. I'm worried about what your parents would think. But we don't have much choice."

"Welcome aboard," said Westley.

Another wave of magical energy passed through them. Jamie sensed that this one was stronger than most of the ones that had passed before.

"We need to go," said Sam. "They're getting close."

Jana nodded. She led the group to the door. She opened the door slowly and took a peek out at the forest. No one was there.

"Let's go," said Jana.

The group left their hiding spot and started jogging up the hill. Their way was hampered by the darkness and the lack of any path. Every once in a while Jamie would feel another wave of magical energy passing through them. She hoped that it was just her fear, but she felt it growing stronger every second.

"Can't we just fly?" said Jamie. "We'll be able to go a lot more quickly."

"No," said Sam. "If you use any magic they'll latch onto it and be able to find us."

The group kept moving. After about ten minutes, Anna slipped and fell down. Her leg hit a rock and opened a large cut on her shin. She cried out in pain and then knelt down, with her hand sliding over the cut. A half-second later, the cut was healed.

"No magic!" warned Jana, but it was too late. A loud sound, unlike any Jamie had heard before, came from behind the group. A second later, a bright light appeared in the sky and started to home in on the group.

"They've found us!" said Jamie.

"We need to fly," said Sam. "I'll distract them."

Sam threw up her hands. Brilliant sparks of light shot forth from the ground about forty feet to the group's right. Jana put her arms under Westley's, and Anna put her arms under Mallory's, and they both began to lift off the ground.

"Hurry!" said Sam. By this time, she was airborne and floating over the group.

Jana and Anna struggled into the air, while Jamie and Sam zoomed around like leaves in the wind. Lights flashed around them, illuminating the tree tops.

"Come on!" said Sam. "We need to move!"

Sam darted around. She had clearly mastered flying to an extent that none of the others had done. She moved quickly, more quickly than anyone could run. Jana and Anna lumbered into flight like large, clumsy animals, dipping and weaving from one side to the other as exhibits to their lack of control.

A light passed by Jana and stopped. Soon, the entire group was bathed in a glaring white light.

"Dive!" said Sam. "To the ground! They've caught us!"

The group fell down to the ground in a hard landing.

"Oof," said Westley.

"Sorry," said Jana.

Even as they landed, the light stayed with the group. Jamie may have been imagining it, but she felt like she was starting to glow.

"They've found us," said Sam.

"We need to sprint," said Jana. "If we run quickly, we might have a chance…"

"Forget it," said Sam. "I've tried this a hundred times. Once they have that light on you, you have maybe a minute and a half until they find you. The glow stays with you."

"Then we're caught?" said Mallory.

Sam nodded.

"Can you teleport us?" asked Jamie of Jana. "Like Vissara did to you?"

"Teleport?" asked Sam.

"She never taught me that spell," said Jana.

"Karsha taught me how to do it," said Anna.

"So get us out of here," said Jamie.

"I've never done more than one thing at once," said Anna. "And then never over land that I didn't know about."

"Hurry," said Westley.

"If I get it wrong," said Anna, "we could end up in the middle of a rock. We'll be dead."

"We'll be dead if they catch us," said Jana. "Do your best."

"I can't," said Anna.

"Just do it," said Jamie.

The leaves started to rustle in the distance. The Vaspen were closing in on the group.

"Anna…" said Jana.

"Quiet!" said Anna. "Okay, everyone join hands."

Everyone huddled together, joining hands with each other.

"Stop!" came a call in the distance. "Stop right there!"

"Pray this works," said Anna.

A moment later Jamie found herself falling from the sky. A fraction of a second later she landed in cool salt water, hitting the sandy bottom in water about three feet deep. She struggled to her feet against an undertow from a wave.

"It worked," said Anna softly.

Jana ran over to Anna and hugged her.

"Good job, sis," said Jana.

"Yeah, thanks," said Jamie.

Westley and Mallory struggled to their feet.

"Where's Sam?" said Jamie.

"I'm here," said Sam as she crawled in from the ocean.

Anna had teleported the group successfully to the original cove. Jamie could see the boat in the moonlight, still hanging off of a rock in the cove. She looked back and saw Jay and Dea on the shore, huddling in a makeshift tent.

"Now," said Jana, "we have to figure out how to get out of here."

"In that?" asked Sam, pointing to the boat.

"Yes," said Jamie.

"There's a hole in the boat," said Jana. "Even if we were to get it off the rock, we wouldn't be able to sail it anywhere. It would just sink."

"Oh," said Sam. "I can fix that. Piece of cake. I just need light."

"Can we wait until the morning?" said Jana.

"I don't know," said Sam. "They might be able to track us here, but chances are they won't be able to get their boats around until the morning. I think we have time."

"Then we'll go tomorrow morning," said Jana.

Chapter Eleven

Beyond the Sea

The night passed without incident. The morning sun arose and the group found themselves busy at work.

"Okay," said Sam. "I could use some help lifting this thing."

"Lifting?" asked Jamie.

"Yeah," said Sam. "Just reach out and help me pick it up. It's heavier than I thought it would be."

"With my hands?" said Jamie.

"No, silly," said Sam. "With magic. Come on. Just imagine that you've got a big pair of hands that can pick it up."

"Okay," said Jana. "I think I see what you mean."

Jana, Anna, Jamie and Sam focused their energies on the boat. A half minute later, it began to lift off the rock it was caught on. Slowly the boat moved its way to the right, over a patch of open ocean.

"Okay," said Sam. "Now set it down gently."

"It's going to sink if we do that," said Anna. "There's a hole in there."

"I'll handle that," said Sam. "Just hold the boat up."

Jamie, Anna and Jana struggled with the magic necessary to hold up the boat. Jamie then watched in amazement as Sam went to work. Slowly the wood surrounding the hole in the boat began to expand inwards, closing the hole. A few minutes later, the boat had been patched and was floating in the cove.

"Quick," said Westley, "get over there and set the anchor before it floats away."

Jana rushed over to Westley and grabbed him. She took to the air. A minute later, the two landed roughly on the deck of the boat.

"Here," said Jana, "you do it. You're better than I am."

Westley nodded and scurried to the back of the boat. He let down an anchor.

"Okay," said Westley, "let's get everyone over here and ready. If we hurry we can probably get out of here in an hour."

The group scurried about. Jana and Anna carried Jay and Dea to the boat. As the sailors prepared the sails, Jana and Anna began carting things from the beach to the boat. Jamie spent her time drawing in the sand.

"What are you doing?" said Sam.

"Just drawing," said Jamie.

"Why?" said Sam.

"It's something I do," said Jamie. "When I need to keep out of people's way."

"Shouldn't we be helping?" asked Sam.

"I don't know," said Jamie. "Maybe."

"The quicker we get out of here, the better," said Sam.

"You're not going to miss this place?" said Jamie.

"I've spent enough time here," said Sam.

"Sometimes I miss my parents," said Jamie.

"Did you leave them too?" said Sam.

"No," said Jamie, "they died."

"I'm sorry," said Sam.

"It was when I first met Jana," said Jamie. "Some guards came to our house, thinking that Jana was hiding there. They killed my parents because they wouldn't say where she was."

"That's horrible," said Sam.

"I was in back," said Jamie, "hiding. I remember feeling a sense of panic. I felt like if they found me that I would have been next. Then Jana showed up."

"What happened?" said Sam.

"She killed the guards," said Jamie. "And then she found me. A few days later, she agreed to mentor me, to teach me magic. Do you have mentors here?"

"We have teachers," said Sam. "They're probably the same thing."

"I wouldn't say Jana's been like a mother to me," said Jamie. "She's never really tried to protect me or stop me from doing something. But she's taught me a lot. She's opened up a whole new world for me."

"Yeah?" said Sam.

"Well," said Jamie, "my parents were poor. We were farmers. Half of the food we grew was confiscated by the king for use by the kingdom, and the other half was barely enough to keep us alive. We didn't ever leave our village, which was a small collection of fifteen or so families who were also farmers. We had nothing."

"Since that time," said Jamie, "I've seen all of the great cities. I've met the king. I've been on the run. I've studied in the royal library. I was in the wedding party for a wedding held at the royal ballroom. I've met a dragon, and helped kill another dragon. I've done things I could never imagine doing."

"That's what I want to do, too," said Sam. "I'm trapped here in this village, just like you were. I can't wait until we leave."

"Even with all that," said Jamie, "I still miss my parents. I wish I could see them again. I wish I could show them what I've done."

"Hm," said Sam. "I won't miss mine."

"Are you sure?" said Jamie.

"Yeah," said Sam. "They hate me."

"Jamie," called Jana, "Come on."

The boat was ready. Jamie dropped her design and flew over to the boat. Sam followed her.

"Anchors away?" asked Westley.

"Not yet," said Jana. She then turned to look at Sam.

"What?" asked Sam.

"I need to know if you're sure you want to do this," said Jana.

"Yes," said Sam.

"We don't have magic where we're going," said Jana. "Most of the things you're used to doing you won't be able to do there."

"I don't care," said Sam.

"I'm not in a position where I can take another apprentice," said Jana, "not that I'd have anything to teach you. You'd be on your own."

"I don't care," said Sam.

"I mean, we're grateful for your help," said Jana. "But we don't want to kid you about what we want. None of us needs an apprentice right now. You would really be on your own, without help, in a land entirely unfamiliar to you."

"I don't care," said Sam. "Can we get on with it?"

"All right," said Jana, "just so you're sure."

"Anchors away?" said Westley.

Jana walked over to Westley and then took a look back at the island.

"No," said Jana.

"No?" said Westley. "Let's get out of here while we can."

"No," said Jana. "I came here to get a hive of flutterbees."

"Jana," said Westley, "no, they'll kill us. We just spent a week imprisoned."

"I don't care," said Jana. "If we leave now all we've done is taken one of their kids. Everything will go on as it had before, except anyone who comes back here will be branded as kidnappers."

"Huh?" said Westley.

"The Vaspen believed in the power of prophecy," said Jana. "Kaseraak had prophecies of his own. There is a prophecy of magic dwindling into irrelevance. There is also a prophecy of magic ascending, helping us create a society without poverty and injustice. Which prophecy comes true depends entirely on what we do right now."

Westley shook his head.

"Come on, sis," said Anna. "We'll be killed if we go back there."

"Maybe," said Jana. "But we knew that coming in. We can't give up now."

Jamie walked over to Jana and grabbed her hand.

"I'm with you," said Jamie.

"Count me in too," said Sam.

"You'll get yourself killed," said Westley.

"If we're not back in two hours," said Jana, "sail off without us."

"You know I can't do that," said Westley.

"You might need to," said Jana.

"I'll watch for trouble," said Mallory. She climbed the aft mast of the boat and perched herself at the top of the sails.

"Let's go," said Jana.

"Oh, all right," said Anna. "I'm sure I'd regret it if you ended up dying and I wasn't there to save you."

"Thanks, sis," Jana said.

Jana, Jamie, Anna and Sam flew back over to the island. They landed in the small field and looked up ahead.

"What's our plan?" whispered Anna.

"Well," said Jana, "we need one of the hives. I figure we can lift it like we did the boat, and then maybe carry it over with us."

"Won't the flutterbees sting us?" said Jamie.

"They only sting if their hive is endangered," said Sam.

"Isn't that exactly what we're doing?" said Jamie.

"Well, I suppose," said Sam.

"I could cast a sleep spell over the hive," said Anna. "We would probably need to in order to get it to the mainland, anyway. The flutterbees won't have any flowers on the way back."

"Okay," said Jana.

"Okay?" said Anna. "I've never tried anything like that."

"We've done a lot of things we've never tried before," said Jana.

"Right," said Anna.

"Okay," said Jana, "once Anna casts her sleep spell, Jamie, what I want you to do is start digging up the ground around it. Give it a good few yards. We don't want to harm the hive at all. Then we'll take the whole thing, dirt, flowers and all, over to the ship."

"Okay," said Jamie.

"Okay," said Anna.

"Let's go," said Jana.

The group snuck through the grass. Fifty yards of walking later, they found a flutterbee hive. It was about five feet tall and buzzing with flutterbees.

"This looks like a good one," said Jana. "Anna, do your stuff."

Anna closed her eyes for a moment, wrinkled her brow and pointed her open hand at the hive. Jamie saw a very slight mist rain down over the hive. As the mist fell, the flutterbees began to buzz more slowly. A minute later, the activity in the hive stopped.

"Okay," said Jana. "Jamie, your turn."

Jamie nodded. Using her digging spell, she dug a trench in a circle around the hive. The circle had a radius of four yards, and Jamie dug about two feet deep into the ground.

"Okay," said Jana after about ten minutes of digging. "We should be able to move it now. Anna, Jamie, Sam, lift it up. I'll keep an eye out."

Jamie concentrated and helped lift up the hive and surrounding ground. After the boat, this was relatively easy for her.

"Let's go slowly," said Jana. "We don't want to drop it."

The group walked down the hill slowly, over toward the cliff's edge. When they were about twenty feet from the edge, a woman dropped from the sky in front of them.

"Stop right there," she said.

Jamie felt the weight of the hive increase as Anna let go of it. Jana stepped in front of the hive and shook her hand, making it come ablaze in fire.

"Do you really think your pathetic magic will protect you here?" the woman said.

"She's bluffing," said Sam. "She won't hurt us."

The woman shot her hand up to the sky, sending forth a bolt of brilliant blue light. Jana sent a ball of fire toward the woman. The woman waved her hand, reflecting the fire away.

"Leave the Vaspen girl," said the woman, "and step away from the hive."

"She won't attack," said Sam. "Not as long as we stay near the hive. Not as long as I'm here."

"I don't need to attack," said the woman.

The woman waved her hands. A glowing shell began to form around the group. Jana thrust her hands forward, sending forth a fireball. The fireball hit the shell and dissipated, the flames crackling throughout the shell.

"See?" said the woman.

Jana tried again. This time, the fireball was much bigger and more powerful. The collision exploded all around them, throwing everyone but Jana to the ground with its force. Jamie heard a shattering noise, much like the breaking of glass. The woman fell to her knees.

Jana pressed her advantage. She shot a quick fireball at the woman. The fireball hit her midsection and knocked the woman to the ground, putting her garments in flame. Jana ran over toward her, with a fireball forming in her left hand.

"Stop!" yelled Sam. She ran over to the woman and hugged her. "Mom!"

"Mom?" said Jamie underneath her breath.

Jana approached the woman and lowered her left hand. Her hand was still ablaze with a fireball, but she didn't appear to be ready to throw it.

"I'm sorry," said Sam, "I'm sorry I ran away, mom. Please don't die. Please don't kill her."

The woman coughed. Jana lowered her hand to her side. The fireball was gone.

"This is your daughter?" said Jana.

The woman coughed again and then nodded.

Six more Vaspen surrounded the group. One of them Jamie recognized as Heather, one of the Vaspen elders.

"I'm sorry," said Jana.

"Stand down," said Heather. "You are surrounded. There is no point in fighting."

Jana looked at Heather. "All right," she said.

"Now what?" said Anna.

"We Vaspen have several prophecies related to your arrival," said Heather. "We have been discussing our own fate for several days now."

"And?" said Jana.

"Our fate is tied not to your mission, Jana Aliston," the woman said, "but rather to this Vaspen child."

"Sam?" said Jamie.

"She is spurred by a desire to rejoin the mainland," said Heather. "But there are several ways of going about that. Were she to have left with you earlier, that would have meant doom for us."

"How can you be sure?" said Jana.

"I have seen that future, now that such a thing could be contemplated," said Heather. "She would arrive in your lands, alone, but without the mastery of magic to lead or command anyone. Her life would become miserable, and her misery would create a resentment of her homeland. Though she would not be involved personally, her resentment would inspire others to invade our island. We would perish in the invasion."

"And the alternative?" asked Anna.

"If she were to stay here," said Heather, "she would still desire a connection with the mainland. She would eventually travel there, but this time with the intent of returning. Ultimately our island's movement would be reversed, and we would set a course to rejoin your society on the mainland."

"Where does that leave us?" asked Jana.

"Your future is irrelevant to the prophecy," said Heather. "Whether you succeed or fail in your mission is ultimately of little concern to us."

"What do we do now, then?" asked Jana.

"Mom?" said Sam.

"Yes?" said Sam's mother.

"Let them go," said Sam. "Can you convince them? Jamie's my friend."

"This is bigger than me," said Sam's mother.

"I told you of our mission," said Jana. "We hope to take a hive to repopulate the mainland with magic."

"Doing so has risks for us," said Heather, "and benefits, but it does not affect our fate one way or the other. You might want to consider how it would affect your own fate, however."

"I've considered," said Jana. "Westvalia will be better off with plentiful magic."

"I was not referring to Westvalia," said Heather. She pointed directly at Anna. "I was referring to you."

"We don't believe in prophecies," said Anna.

"Then," said Heather, "you will likely be doomed to suffer from flawed decisions."

"Let them go," said Sam, this time directly to Heather.

Heather looked at Sam, then up at Jana and Jamie, then back to Sam again.

"All right," said Heather after a moment's thought. "Since it does not matter to our future, let us be graceful and send them on their way. They may take one hive."

"Thank you," said Jana.

Heather looked at Jana and frowned. "I would not think you would be thanking me. But I have forgotten that your future has not been prophesized by you."

Jana shook her head. "I don't believe in that anyway."

Sam walked up to Jamie and held her hands.

"I guess this is goodbye, then," said Sam.

"Yeah," said Jamie.

"You've been the best friend I've ever had," said Sam.

"You've only known me for a week," said Jamie.

"But you've opened up new possibilities," said Sam. "You made me see a world I would have only imagined. And you were there for me when no one else was."

"Thanks," said Jamie, "I think. And thanks for saving us."

Sam walked up to Jamie and kissed her on the cheek. She then hugged her tight.

"I'll miss you," said Sam.

"I'll miss you too," said Jamie.

"And don't worry," said Sam as she stepped back. "We will see each other again."

"We will?" asked Jamie.

"It's fate," said Sam.

"Come on, sprite," said Jana. "Let's go."

Jana, Jamie and Anna floated into the air, carrying the flutterbee hive with them. After they were about half way to the boat, Jamie turned back. Sam was still there watching her. Jamie waved goodbye.

Sam waved back.

"Goodbye," said Jamie, though she didn't say it loudly enough for anyone else to hear it.

Chapter Twelve

Return of the Flutterbee

"Anchors away?" said Westley as Jana returned to the boat.

Jana nodded. "Anchors away."

"Finally," said Westley.

"Sail for Westvalia," said Jana.

"With good wind," said Westley, "we'll be there in five days."

The voyage back was uneventful. Jamie watched the flutterbees closely. Occasionally one our two would buzz to the surface of the hive, but the sleep spell Anna had put on them made them so groggy as to be unable to fly away from the hive.

As the boat left the Cuttyhunk Islands, Jamie noticed almost immediately the drop in magical energy. She felt weak without it. She didn't think the sleeping flutterbees were generating any magic, but it might have been that she was so used to the strength of the magic on the island that the magic on the boat was still relatively strong, compared with the mainland. She had lost her frame of reference.

After a week's worth of sailing, the boat arrived in Westvalia's harbor. The harbor was a few miles away from the city proper, but it had the bustle of the central markets in the city. Several other boats were docked at the various piers, with workers loading and unloading goods.

As Jana stepped off the boat onto the pier, she was greeted by a familiar and exceptionally large royal guard.

"Miss Aliston," said the guard.

"Oh," said Jana, "you again."

"The king sends his regards," said the guard. "He will be most pleased to learn of your return."

"I'm sure," said Jana.

"I am instructed to ask you whether your trip was successful," said the guard.

"Yes," said Jana, "yes it was."

"The king will be pleased," said the guard.

"Good," said Jana.

"Yes," said the guard.

"Is there anything else?" asked Jana.

"No," said the guard. "There is very specifically nothing else for me to say to you."

"Okay," said Jana with her head cocked slightly to her side.

"Even more specifically," the guard said, "there is not a wagon here waiting for you. The king reiterates his position of neutrality with respect to your mission."

Jana nodded. Just beyond the guard she noticed a wagon tied to a very healthy horse. Presumably it was the one that was not waiting for her.

"Very well," said Jana. "Send my best regards to the king. Very specifically, though, you should not thank him for his failure to help me."

Jana winked. The guard nodded.

"As you were," the guard said. He walked away.

"What was that about?" Jamie asked Jana.

"Oh," said Jana, "remember how Tybilt said he can't officially support what I was doing? I think he wants to help us but he doesn't want to be seen as helping the dragons in any way. So he can't be offering us a wagon to help us transport the hive."

"But here it is," said Jamie.

"Yes," said Jana. "And remember, you have no idea where this came from."

Jamie nodded. She finally understood.

"Come on," said Jana. "We have to get the hive."

Jana grabbed the reins of the horse and led him onto the pier next to the boat.

"All right, sprite," said Jana. "Time to see how much they help our magic. Let's lift the hive onto the wagon."

Jamie nodded. She followed along with Jana as the two used their magic together to lift the hive. It felt heavy, but not nearly as heavy as the boat when she helped lift that. Jamie felt confident that she could do it alone. A few moments later, the hive was in place on the wagon.

"I guess this is goodbye, then," said Westley after the hive was loaded.

"For now," said Jana. "Are you shipping out right away?"

"No," said Westley. "We've arranged a load to haul back to Hockessin. It should take the boys a few days to load everything up, and then we'll be on our way. But I do need to stay around here to keep an eye on it."

"Well," said Jana, "next time you're in port, come in to the city proper. I'll show you around."

"I'd like that," said Westley.

"Take care of yourself, sprite," Mallory said to Jamie.

"I'll try," said Jamie.

"Do you miss her?" Mallory said.

"Who?" said Jamie.

"Sam," said Mallory.

"Yeah, I guess," she said. "It was nice to be able to hang around with someone my age for a change."

"Well," said Mallory, "if you ever want to learn some hunting tricks, look me up."

"I will," said Jamie.

That left Anna.

"I'm heading back to Hockessin on the boat," said Anna.

"Do you want to come with us to set the flutterbees free?" asked Jana. "We could probably use your help."

"That's okay," said Anna. "I'm sure you guys will be fine. I have a few things I need to check in on in the city anyway."

"Are you sure?" asked Jana.

"Yeah," said Anna.

Jana frowned.

"Hey," said Anna, "how about we meet up tomorrow night for dinner? You should be done with setting the flutterbees free by then, shouldn't you?"

"Yes," said Jana. "That sounds fine."

"And Westley and Mallory can come too," said Anna. "It'll be a nice cap to this grand adventure."

"Sounds good," said Jana.

Anna hugged Jana and then Jamie. Jana took the horse's reins and began walking it away from the pier, the wagon with the flutterbee hive following slowly behind them. They started on the road toward Theoton, a road that ran south from the port and would follow the coast for the most of the way toward that city. Jana and Jamie had no intention of following it that far. In a few miles, they planned on taking a side road which led into the southwestern plains. Jana planned on being about fifteen miles inland before setting the flutterbees loose. She figured they would be in a good spot mid-afternoon. Anna said that, without her keeping the sleep spell active, the flutterbees would wake up in a couple of days.

About a half hour into their journey, Jana and Jamie were joined by a handsome young man.

"May I walk with you for a while?" the young man said.

"Certainly," said Jana.

The young man was such that Jamie, were she not already prepared for this eventuality, would be completely smitten. She had seen such a young man before, and had been burned by her affections to him. She recognized that he wasn't a young man at all, but instead was an avatar: a projection spell used by an ancient dragon, much like the one she had used as a mouse on the island.

"There are some matters I would wish to discuss with you," the man said.

146

"I'm sure you do, Ceredos," Jana said.

"Am I that transparent?" the young man said.

"Yes," said Jana in utter seriousness. Jamie had to stifle a giggle.

"It appears that you will succeed in your mission," said Ceredos. "The flutterbee hive looks healthy, and should be able to multiply throughout the plains within a matter of decades. You have done well."

"Thank you," said Jana.

"As you have held to your end of the bargain, I will hold to mine," said Ceredos. "In six months time the ancient dragons will hold council. I will inform them of your deeds and we will consider ourselves at peace with your human kingdom."

"Good," said Jana.

"Did you have much difficulty obtaining the hive?" said Ceredos.

"No," said Jana. "It was a piece of cake."

Jamie blinked twice at the baldfaced lie.

"I'm glad to hear that," said Ceredos. "Well, I will be on my way then."

"Very well," said Jana. "Take care."

Ceredos slowed his pace until he was behind the wagon.

"Why did you lie to him?" said Jamie.

"Shh," said Jana. "He's still following us."

"Okay," said Jamie a bit less loudly. "Why did you lie to him about how difficult it was to get the hive."

"They've never played straight with me," said Jana. "They lied to me about the island and the reason why they couldn't get the hive. Why should I be straightforward with them?"

"Isn't it usually a good thing?" said Jamie.

"He probably knows I'm lying," said Jana. "Chances are he knew it would be terrifically difficult. The thing is, he understated the difficulties we would face. If I tell him how difficult it actually was, that makes him think I have less power than I could project by claiming that he was right all along. Do you understand?"

"No," said Jamie. She thought Jana was speaking a foreign language.

"Let's simplify," said Jana. "He said it was going to be easy, knowing that it would be tough. That assumes one set of abilities from me. If I confirm for him that it was tough, it confirms that suspicion. If I say it was easy, though, he has to be wary of me."

"So you want him to be wary of you?" said Jamie.

"Yes," said Jana. "I want them to be afraid."

"Why?" said Jamie.

"Because," said Jana, "we've just given up a big chip. There still could be war. We don't know. And yes, he is still following us."

Jana and Jamie walked ahead for another half hour. Every once in a while, Jamie would look over her shoulder. Ceredos's avatar was still following them each time.

"How long do you think he'll follow us?" said Jamie.

"Until we're done, sprite," said Jana.

"All the way there?" said Jamie.

"All the way there," said Jana.

Jamie sighed and shrugged. She didn't like dragon avatars. She kept marching forward, up a slight incline toward what seemed to be endless rolling plains ahead. After another hour's walk, she was treated to some new scenery. She could see a barn in the distance. On a closer look it seemed to be abandoned, but it was the first sign of human life she had seen since leaving the port area and entering the plains. She snuck another glance behind her, trying not to get caught looking.

Ceredos was no longer there.

Jamie turned around and stopped walking. She wondered if he had just stumbled for a bit. She didn't see him. After getting about fifteen paces ahead, Jana stopped the horse and waited for Jamie.

"What is it?" said Jana.

"Ceredos is gone," said Jamie. She felt sure that he would have appeared by now if he were still following them.

"Maybe he trusts us now," said Jana.

"Maybe," said Jamie.

"Or maybe he's just assumed a smaller form," said Jana. "Like a mouse."

"I don't think so," said Jamie. "They seem to delight in being seen."

"Maybe," said Jana. She shrugged. "Either way, let's keep going. It doesn't matter."

"Okay," said Jamie.

"Let's take a rest at this barn up here," said Jana.

"Okay," said Jamie.

The barn was another five minutes walk ahead. When Jana and Jamie arrived there, Jana hitched the horse to a post and then sat down.

"We're almost there, sprite," said Jana.

"Why do we have to go so far, anyway?" said Jamie.

"If the flutterbees are too close to a city," Jana said, "they might die off rather than spread through the land. Ideally I'd want to place them in the middle of all these plains, but I don't have the patience for that."

"Okay," said Jamie.

"We're close," said Jana. "A couple more hours should do it. But for now let's take a few moments in the shade, give the horse a bit of a rest, and let's go."

"Okay," said Jamie.

Jamie walked around the barn. It seemed like it had been something that was used within the past decade, but abandoned since then. Jamie thought of a building that she and Jana had discovered a couple of years ago. That building had been constructed by Westvalia to create poison, and it was constructed to look old, much as this one was.

Jamie sat down and took a deep breath. She could feel the magic of the flutterbees getting to her. It felt good. After a few minutes rest, she stood back up and walked over to the horse. When she got there, she saw that someone else had joined Jana.

"Oh," said Sylvia, "hello Jamie. How are you?"

Chapter Thirteen

Persuasion

"You," said Jamie. "How did you get here?"

"I followed you, of course," said Sylvia. "I missed you both!"

"Why are you here?" said Jana.

"Oh, come on now," said Sylvia. "You should know better than to ask me that by now."

"What?" said Jana.

"Come on," said Sylvia. "You both left the city without word about a month and a half ago. It took a bit of asking around to find out where you had went, and a bit more persuading to learn what you were up to. I learned that you had spoken with a dragon."

"I can't imagine that it was much of a surprise," said Jana. "I'd think half the city knew that."

"You'd be surprised, my dear," said Sylvia. "Still, that was easy information to get. What was harder to get was the content of your discussion. Turns out only a few people knew that."

"And?" said Jana.

"Some of Tybilt's most trusted guards," said Sylvia. "They witnessed your meeting with him, and one eventually told me all I needed to know. His name was Seth. A sweet boy, that Seth."

"What did you do to him?" asked Jamie.

"Don't you worry about Seth," said Sylvia. She walked up to the horse and rubbed it on the nose. "All I did was persuade him to tell me what happened. And as you know, I can be quite persuasive."

"What did he tell you?" said Jana.

"Why, you should know what he told me," said Sylvia. "You've been there for a month and a half. Off you sailed from Hockessin toward the southern seas, off to recover a flutterbee hive. I take it that's what this thing is?"

"Yes," said Jana.

"Excellent," said Sylvia. "Why did the dragons want this?"

"I don't know," said Jana.

"Don't lie to me, Jana," Sylvia said. "You know better than that. You know that I can pluck the truth from you like a feather from a chicken."

"They said it had something to do with their reproduction," said Jana. "But I've learned not to trust what ancient dragons tell me."

"Very wise," said Sylvia. "But it doesn't matter why they want it. All that matters is that they want it, and something like that I can take advantage of."

"What?" said Jamie.

"What are you proposing?" said Jana.

"It's quite simple, really," said Sylvia. "If you were to take the hive and set it in the fields a few miles southwest of here, you would lose control of it. Whatever the dragons wanted with it, they could get. Now that they had that, they would feel no particular need to keep their bargain with you. The dragons could wipe human civilization clean without worry for their own future."

"I would stand to stop them," said Jana.

"You would think you would, Jana," said Sylvia. "Yet when the time came to decide, you chose the fictional allure of the savior of magic over the safety of your own cities. Undoubtedly the dragons could trick you again, if they felt it necessary. As it was, you risked life and limb to bring the very thing they needed for their own survival."

"I didn't do that for them," said Jana. "I brought the flutterbee hive back because it would help our society claim the greatness only abundant magic can give it."

"You keep telling yourself that," said Sylvia. "You would have never gone to those islands by yourself. You would have never done any of that unless you were asked. Just like you would not have gone after Norzakind unless Tybilt asked you, or done any of the things you've done because Kaseraak wanted you to do."

Jana shook her head.

"It's okay Jana," said Sylvia. "It's who you are. It's past time you admitted that."

Sylvia walked up to Jana and hugged her. Jana was slow to react, but she eventually returned the embrace.

"Good," Sylvia said, "that's good my dear. Why don't we take this wagon into the barn and we can discuss what to do next?"

"Okay," said Jana.

Jamie blinked. She looked back and forth between Sylvia and Jana as if something were completely wrong. Something about the exchange rankled her.

"Come on," Sylvia said to Jamie. "Let's go inside."

Jamie shrugged. There wasn't much point in objecting.

Sylvia went to open the barn door. Jana led the horse inside. When the wagon was fully inside the barn, Sylvia closed the door behind it. The barn was mostly dark, but light snuck through the holes in the roof. The shape and change of those holes changed with the breeze, creating an uncertain dance of light overhead.

"It's dark," said Jamie.

"Aren't old barns wonderful?" said Sylvia. "The light plays around with the shadows on the walls, and you can imagine any number of wonderful things."

"Uh, yeah," said Jamie. She backed off into a corner of the barn.

"And now we wait," said Sylvia. "The dragon is sure to investigate the destruction of his avatar. With any luck he will fly here personally. Then we can destroy him as we did Norzakind."

"We had a rough time of it fighting Norzakind," said Jana.

"That is because I was foolish," said Sylvia. "I went in unprepared for her defenses to my spells. I was blind to my own weaknesses. My resolve is stronger now, and I have a strategy now. This time I will not fail you, Jana. This time I will take down the dragon."

"We don't need to do that," said Jamie.

"Of course we need to do it, child," Sylvia said. "Having the flutterbee hive is the one advantage we have over the dragons. He won't dare attack us directly for fear of harming the flutterbees. On the other hand, once we relinquish control of the flutterbees, the dragons will have every reason to attack to maintain their dominance over humanity."

"I don't think they would do that," said Jamie.

"Of course not, dear," said Sylvia. "You wouldn't think that because for some reason you still trust the dragons. I've learned differently. And so has Jana."

Sylvia smiled at Jana. Jana sighed heavily.

"She's right, sprite," Jana said.

"But..." said Jamie.

"It all makes sense," said Jana.

"They fooled you again," said Sylvia. "They got you to go off and get the one thing they needed, the one thing for whatever reason they couldn't get themselves. You convinced yourself that you were doing it for yourself, much like you convinced yourself that you killed Norzakind for your own reasons. You had those reasons, but they weren't what motivated you, were they?"

"No," said Jana.

"That's all right, dear," said Sylvia. She walked over to Jana and grasped her hand. "You've been running other people's errands for all your life now. Now it's time for you to seize control back from the dragons. Now's the time for you to exact payment."

Jana nodded. Jamie looked over at her and yelped.

"Jana!" said Jamie. "Come over here," she said, almost reaching out to tug her into the corner of the barn where Jamie was huddled.

"Sure, sprite," Jana said. She walked over to the corner. Sylvia watched every step with a grin on her face.

"Are you okay?" said Jamie under her breath.

"What?" said Jana.

"You know," said Jamie. "Sometimes she gets like this, and, well, you kind of lose it."

"You mean she persuades me?" said Jana.

"If that's what you want to call it," said Jamie. "It's unnatural."

Sylvia laughed and walked over to the pair of them. Jamie shut up and looked up at her, trying to crawl back further into the wall.

"You think I am using my magic to convince her?" said Sylvia.

Sylvia placed her hand on Jana's shoulder. A chill filled the air. Jamie looked at Jana. Jana's face was expressionless, as if she had been frozen in time. She looked back to Sylvia in horror.

"I could do that," said Sylvia. "I could do that very easily. Watch."

Jamie tried to push herself back through the wall as she watch Sylvia caress Jana's cheek with her hand. Jana's face remained stoic, unblinking and seemingly unaware of her circumstance.

"Jana dearest," said Sylvia, "shall we kill the bad dragons?"

"Yes," said Jana almost robotically.

"That's a good dear," Sylvia said. "You know, Jamie, sometimes I wonder why I don't just do this. I could ask her the question I've been wanting to ask her for years."

Jamie curled up in the corner. She wanted to turn away, but she found her eyes fixed on Jana.

"Jana, would you like to become my apprentice now?" Sylvia laughed softly as she ran a nail along the side of Jana's neck.

"Yes, Sycosina," Jana said, again almost robotically. "I would like to become your apprentice."

"Are you sure?" Sylvia said. She grasped Jana's throat with both her hands and rested her chin upon Jana's shoulder. "One flick of my wrist is all it would take."

"No," cried Jamie. She tried to reach to stop her.

"Yes," said Jana. "Do it."

"Not right now, dear," Sylvia said. She dragged her arms down Jana's back and walked away from her with a slight laugh.

Jamie took a huge breath of relief.

"Sometimes I wonder why I haven't done that before," said Sylvia. "It would be all too easy."

Sylvia snapped her fingers. Jana shook her head slowly, apparently not responding to anything Sylvia had just done.

"Yes, child," said Sylvia. "I do have that power of persuasion. I could simply seduce you both into following my every wish. But I don't do that. I don't do that because you are my friends, and I don't do that because I value your honest opinions and effort."

"She's right," said Jana.

"But Jana," Jamie said, "she had her fingers at your throat. She could have turned you into her apprentice."

"But she wouldn't," said Jana.

"But," said Jamie.

"You're going to have to get over your fear of me," said Sylvia.

"But," said Jamie.

"She's right," Jana said. "About the strategy. We would give up too much by just letting the flutterbees go free without extracting some information from the dragons. We need to plan something."

Sylvia patted Jana on the shoulder and smiled.

"Precisely," said Sylvia. "We can't just give the dragons what they need without some form of payment."

"But this isn't about you," said Jamie. "You didn't go to the island to get the flutterbees with us."

"A thousand thousand souls cry out," said Sylvia, "and I am the instrument of their vengeance. Anything having to do with the dragons has to do with me."

"She's right," said Jana. "This involves her just as much as it does us."

The ceiling of the barn darkened for a split second. A moment later, rushing wind clattered at the boards of the barn.

"He's here," said Sylvia. "Go out and talk to him. I need a little bit of time."

"What do I say?" said Jana. Jamie looked startled for a second. She wondered if Jana were still under Sylvia's thrall. Never before had Jana seemed so willing to cede control over a situation.

"Just keep him talking," said Sylvia. "I'll need about five minutes."

"Then what?" said Jamie.

"After that," said Sylvia, "duck."

Chapter Fourteen

Dragon Soul

Jana and Jamie stepped out onto the road, sliding the barn door open slightly. They stood outside the barn and looked up at the sky. For a second, Jamie thought she might have been wrong to think that a dragon had passed overhead. In that time the dragon swooped overhead again and came to a hard landing in front of the barn.

"Ceredos," Jana said.

The dragon turned around and looked at Jana. He didn't look happy to Jamie, but upon reflection Jamie was never sure that she had ever seen a happy dragon.

"You lost my avatar," said Ceredos.

"I did?" said Jana.

"Don't play coy," said Ceredos. "You knew I was tailing you. I saw your apprentice check over her shoulder every ten minutes or so."

"Why were you following me?" asked Jana.

"Why do you think?" said Ceredos. "I have a vested interest in the safety of that flutterbee hive. I want to make sure it gets to where it is needed."

"Then why not just come directly?" said Jana.

"Have you ever seen what people do when they see an undisguised dragon?" said Ceredos. "We act with avatars because we can do so without notice. This situation is no different."

"Perhaps you are right," said Jana.

"So where is the hive?" said Ceredos.

"It's inside the barn," said Jana.

"May I see it?" asked Ceredos.

"No, you may not," said Jana.

"Why not?" said Ceredos.

"We are giving the horse a rest after a hard morning's work pulling the hive up from the harbor," Jana said. "We were taking such a rest also until you showed up."

"I want to see the hive," said Ceredos.

"Then you will just have to wait," said Jana. "You've spoiled our rest. Hopefully the horse will have better luck ignoring you. It needs the rest."

"I don't care much for your tone," said Ceredos.

"I don't like being spied on," said Jana.

"You knew I would want to," said Ceredos.

"Yes," said Jana, "just as you knew that you were holding something back about that island. You never mentioned the dragons' attacks on that island."

"What attacks?" said Ceredos.

"Your sisters and brothers attacked the island several hundred years ago," said Jana, "quite possibly in an attempt to do exactly what we just did."

"We did no such thing," said Ceredos.

"Don't lie to me," said Jana. "We saw the bones."

"It was never our intent to attack that island," said Ceredos.

"How do you know?" said Jana. "Were you there?"

"Actually," said Ceredos, "I was. I remember wishing my sisters and brothers good luck as they flew south into the southern seas. I waited years for them to return. We feared the worst."

"You're wrong," said Jana.

"That is not how we dragons operate," said Ceredos. "We do not simply attack other living beings, not unless all other options have been exhausted."

"Lies!" came a yell from the barn.

The barn doors burst open. Sylvia stood in the doorway. Her hair flew up into the air as the winds swirled around her. Her left hand was pointed toward the dragon and glowed a sickly green. Her right arm was tucked close to her body. It held a small figurine.

"Who the hell are you?" Ceredos said.

"I am the embodiment of a thousand thousand souls," Sylvia said. "Their cries are mine. And they cry for vengeance."

Green lightning shot forth from Sylvia's hand. With surprising swiftness, Ceredos dodged the blast. He backed up and let loose a warning blast of flame from his mouth, scorching the ground in front of the barn. He began to hover over the road.

"Foolish mortal," said Ceredos. "You dare attack me?"

Ceredos soared skyward. Jamie followed the dragon with her eyes as it looped far in the sky and came in low, over the road. The dragon flew toward the area in front of the barn, about ten feet off the ground, scorching the road with a constant stream of fire. He was headed directly for Sylvia.

"Jana!" said Jamie. "Help!"

"Bring him down," said Sylvia, in defiance of her impending doom.

Jana leapt forward. She grabbed Jamie and ducked at Sylvia's feet. Jana extended a barrier spell around the three of them.

Sylvia held her hand up into the air as the dragon's flames began to engulf her.

"With my fury I leash thee," she said. She pulled down hard on her right hand. Jamie watched in amazement as Ceredos's neck was wrenched backwards. The dragon did a somersault over its head and then crash landed behind them.

Ceredos cried out from his ugly crash. Bones shattered in place. He tried to wobble toward his feet to stand, but got nowhere. He moaned in place.

"You think you are suffering now, dragon?" said Sylvia. "Your suffering has only begun. Jana, hold him down."

"What?" asked Jamie.

Jana waved her hands. The dragons wings became pinned to the ground. Ceredos stopped moving, apparently constricted by Jana's binds.

"I have done nothing to you," said Ceredos through gritted teeth.

"A thousand thousand souls claim otherwise, dragon," Sylvia said. "The souls of the Vaspen were restless after you defeated them. For millennia they could find neither peace nor salvation. Until they found me. They found in me a vessel for vengeance, a tool to reap their fury against those that had destroyed them without mercy. I speak for all of those souls now."

Jamie gulped.

"Who am I?" said Sylvia. "I am Sycosina Soulbane. I am your doom."

Sylvia pointed her left arm at the dragon. A dark yellowish-green mist shot from her arm and began to envelop the dragon. Ceredos started wailing in pain.

"Stop! You must stop!" Ceredos said.

"Oh no," said Sylvia. "I cannot let you feel the full anguish of a thousand thousand souls, not completely, but you will feel that anguish for millenia to come."

"Jana Aliston," said Ceredos. "Stop her."

"Stop me?" Sylvia said with a laugh. "She is helping me. She has come to understand the treachery of the ancient dragons. Perhaps you should have been honest with her when you sent her to that island. Perhaps then she would have been more willing to come to your aid."

Ceredos shrieked in pain. Jamie stumbled backwards and noticed the barn had caught fire. She tried to figure out what she could do to put it out. She tried pulling magical energy away from the barn, sort of like casting a fireball in reverse. That seemed to slow the fire's progress but it didn't completely stop it.

"Jana," said Jamie, "the flutterbees…" It wasn't enough to catch Jana's attention.

"Please…" Ceredos begged pathetically. He was encased in a light blue glow.

"There will be no aid for you, dragon," said Sylvia. "A thousand thousand souls suffered from your cruelty for five thousand years. I think it fitting that you be made to suffer five thousand thousand years for their pain."

"No!" said Ceredos.

The light blue glow flowed away from Ceredos toward Sylvia. Jamie watched in horror as she saw the mist-like glow flow into the crystal Sycosina held in her right hand. The dragon seemed to grow paler by the second. Jamie imagined that the dragon's soul was being drained from his body into the crystal, which was more or less the truth. She thought it was unspeakably horrid.

The dragon fell silent. About a minute later, the blue glow faded from his body. His body still twitched in pain, and his lungs raised and fell with ragged breathing. But the body did not otherwise move, and Jamie felt that his presence was gone.

"Jana, the flutterbees!" Jamie said.

Jana's attention shifted from the dragon to the barn. The fire was growing. Jana waved her hand to cast a spell on the barn. The fire seemed to ease up somewhat, but it didn't stop completely.

"That's dragon flame," said Jana. "I can't put it out, not completely. We need to get the horse out of there."

Jana and Jamie rushed into the barn. Several minutes later, they were leading the horse out of the barn, stepping quickly to avoid the flames that were destroying the barn's frame. They took the wagon a safe distance from the barn and watched it burn.

Sylvia walked up to the pair. Her face was drenched in sweat and her posture was that of one exhausted by strenuous physical exercise. She wore a broad grin on her face.

"What did you do to that dragon?" asked Jamie.

"I did exactly what I said I did," said Sylvia. "That dragon's soul now resides in this crystal, where it will sit for five thousand thousand years. Perhaps longer."

"He's still alive," said Jana.

"His body is a soulless shell," said Sylvia. "He may be like that for a few days. Without the soul, however, it will eventually starve."

"That's evil!" said Jamie. "That's cruel!"

"Was it any more cruel than what the dragons did to us?" said Sylvia.

"'Us'?" said Jamie.

"I speak for the thousand thousand souls that inhabit my being," said Sylvia. "I give them voice."

"Jana," said Jamie, "we need to stop her. This is wrong."

"I'm inclined to agree," said Jana. "We need to talk about this, Sylvia."

"Don't start being the coward on me," said Sylvia. "Wasn't it you who said that Hockessin needed to win its freedom by hitting back against Tybilt, hitting hard enough that Tybilt could no longer ignore it? Isn't that how you won Hockessin's freedom?"

"Yes, but..." Jana said.

"So too must we hit back against the dragons," said Sylvia. "They must come to know the fear that is being subject to the mercy of a foe greater than they. They must come to fear what it is we can do."

"That much is fine," said Jana. "But you're not just hitting back against them. You're seeking bloody revenge for deeds that are long past, deeds that should have long since been forgiven."

"Forgiven?" said Sylvia. "There is no forgiving to be done, not anymore. My restless souls scream to me. We will teach the dragons one by one the pain we have suffered."

"Listen to yourself," said Jana. "You've lost control. Don't you remember who you are?"

"I know who I am," said Sylvia. "I am Sycosina Soulbane. I am the vengeance of a dead people."

"Stop this," said Jana. "You need to control those voices, Sylvia."

"I am those voices," said Sylvia.

"I can't let you do this," said Jana.

"Let me?" said Sylvia. "My dear Jana, not only will you let me. You will help me."

"No," said Jana. "I won't."

Jana braced herself for an attack, but Sylvia's response surprised her. Sylvia walked up to her and touched her cheek softly.

"You will help me," said Sylvia. "I think it's time we made due on all those favors I've done for you."

"No!" said Jamie. She took a step toward Jana but was blasted back by a gust of wind. She found herself pinned to the ground.

"Stay out of this, child," Sylvia said. "This is not your fight."

"Let her go," said Jana through gritted teeth.

"Ah, you are resisting," said Sylvia. "There is little point to that."

Sylvia grasped both of Jana's cheeks with her hands.

"Stop this," said Jana. "Remember who you are."

"Remember who you are," said Sylvia. "You once begged me to let you become my apprentice. Now it is time."

Sylvia walked around to Jana's back. Jana remained motionless.

"I don't want to become your apprentice," said Jana.

"That is only because I have not persuaded you yet."

Sylvia placed her hands on Jana's shoulders and pressed her body against Jana's back.

"No," said Jana.

"Be a good dear," said Sylvia, "and get on your knees."

Sylvia pushed Jana's shoulders down gently. Jana struggled to remain standing, but it was clear that the effort would be futile. She dropped to one knee.

"That's it, my dear," said Sylvia. She began combing her hands through Jana's hair.

"You would never take the unwilling," said Jana.

"True," said Sylvia. "Lower your other knee."

Jana struggled, but she could not resist for long. Her other knee fell to the ground. Jamie wanted to scream out for help, but found that she could do nothing.

"I would never take the unwilling," said Sylvia, "but that does not mean I won't convince you to be willing."

Sylvia let go of Jana's hair and walked around to face her again. She walked up to her and embraced her, pushing Jana's head into her own stomach.

"Now, Jana," said Sylvia. "Shall we remake this world together?"

"Not today," said Jana.

"Don't you see that it is futile to resist me?" said Sylvia. "You are on your knees. Your body listens to my commands. Your mind will soon follow. You know in your heart you want to follow my strength. Let go of your facade of responsibility."

"No, no," said Jana, her voice now cracking.

Sylvia let go of Jana and dropped to her own knees. She cradled Jana's head in her hands and pushed her own head forward, gently touching her forehead to Jana's.

"You wish to join me now," said Sylvia. "Say it."

"I…" Jana said with a stammer. "I want to join you."

Jamie wanted to scream out "no" but her voice was lost in the wind.

"Good girl," said Sylvia. "Say it again."

"I want to become your apprentice," said Jana.

"That's a good dear," said Sylvia.

Sylvia patted Jana on the cheek. She stood up and walked around Jana's body. She stood directly behind her and grasped Jana again, this time by the neck, her sharp fingernails dragging against Jana's skin.

"Say it a third time," said Sylvia, "and it will be done."

"Unhand my sister!" came a yell from the distance.

A fireball exploded next to Jana. The force of the explosion threw Sylvia and Jana back, and forced Sylvia to let go of Jana. Sylvia looked up with a snarl.

"You!" Sylvia said.

"Let her go," said Anna.

"She does not want to be let go," said Sylvia. "She wants to join me."

Jana mumbled and fell to the ground. She seemed weak, almost drained.

"Like hell she does," said Anna. "I'm not going to let that happen."

"There's not much you can do about it," said Sylvia.

"I can do this," said Anna.

Anna's hand burst into flame. With a quick motion, a fireball jumped from her hands and shot at Sylvia. Sylvia dove to the side and the fireball missed her.

"Fool," said Sylvia. "I like Jana, which is why I will let her join me. You I have no such liking for."

Sylvia pointed her hand at Jana. A bright blue bolt of energy shot at Anna. Anna threw up a magical shield to deflect the bolt, but its force knocked her to the ground.

"You can never beat me," said Sylvia.

"I can try," said Anna.

From her knees Anna let loose another ball of fire. This one flew past Sylvia on its own.

"You're already sloppy," said Sylvia.

"Am I?" said Anna.

The ball of fire curved behind Sylvia and came back toward her. Sylvia raised her left hand and deflected the fireball to the ground without even looking at it.

"I've seen that trick before," said Sylvia.

"Have you seen this one?" said Anna.

A strong gust of wind picked up behind Sylvia and spiraled around her. Sylvia was thrown sideways slightly, but rolled away from it and looked at Anna again.

"Sylvia," said Jana weakly. "Stop this."

"You're right, Jana," said Sylvia. "I've toyed with her long enough."

With both her hands, Sylvia shot a constant stream of blue light at Anna. Anna cast a protective shield, but was knocked to her knees. The blue light danced around the shield, crackling and defining it.

"Help!" said Anna.

"She cannot help you," said Sylvia. "She is all but mine."

"Sylvia," said Jana, "stop this. Please. Remember who you are."

"I am Sycosina Soulbane," said Sylvia. "I will remake this world."

"No you aren't," said Jana. "You're Sylvia Sabane. You are my friend."

The shield around Anna began collapsing. Filaments of blue light began to break through the shield and reach her body.

"I am the vengeance of a thousand thousand souls!" said Sylvia.

"No you aren't," said Jana. "You're a young girl, one who suffered an unspeakable tragedy and was granted powers she neither wanted nor comprehended. You wanted to use those powers to right wrongs."

Anna's shield began to collapse. The blue light hit her body and was spreading through it.

"I will avenge their deaths," said Sylvia.

"Not this way," said Jana. "You are letting the spirits control you and that is not who you are. Fight back. Please. Become my friend once again."

Anna's shield collapsed completely. Her body began to convulse in the blue light.

"I am power!" said Sylvia.

"You are my friend," said Jana. "Be my friend, not this."

A few seconds passed.

"Please," said Jana.

Sylvia screamed. The blue beam of light stopped flowing from her hands.

"Out!" yelled Sylvia.

Sylvia screamed again and fell to the ground. A foul odor filled the air. A dark green smoke emerged from Sylvia's body and swirled around her. She fell to her knees, and then over onto the ground. The air yowled in pain.

A moment later, Jamie felt the force gripping her release. Jana fell onto her side. Jamie ran over to Anna. She wasn't moving. She wasn't breathing.

"Anna," said Jamie softly as she broke into tears. "No. No."

Jana crawled to her feet and walked over to Anna. Jana sat down beside her and lifted her chest up. She hugged her sister, but her sister did not hug her back.

Anna Aliston was dead.

Chapter Fifteen

The End

The sun moved westward a few inches. Jana, Anna and Jamie remained in an embrace. Near the road, a horse neighed softly. The flutterbees began to buzz, slowly becoming freed from their magically induced sleep.

"I'm sorry."

The voice was of a young woman. Sylvia stood over Jana, Anna, and Jamie. She frowned.

"Is she…" Sylvia asked.

"She's gone," said Jana. "My little sister is dead."

"Jana, I…" said Sylvia.

"It wasn't you," said Jana. "I know that. She fought to rid you of that curse, just as I did, and just as I know you did."

"The curse is gone," said Sylvia. "The voices of the souls of the past have left."

Jana let Anna rest on the ground. She stood up to face Sylvia.

"I'm sorry," said Sylvia. "I'm so, so sorry."

"I know," said Jana. "I know."

Jana reached out to Sylvia and hugged her hard. Sylvia hugged her back.

Several minutes passed. Eventually Jana went over to the wagon. She unhitched the wagon from the horse and pushed it into the field.

"This will have to do," said Jana.

Jamie nodded. "They'll be fine."

Jana picked Anna's body up. With Jamie's help, Jana placed her sister's body on the horse.

"Let's go," said Jana.

"What about the dragon?" said Jamie.

Jana looked at the dragon. It was still breathing and twitching. Jana looked to Sylvia.

"Give me the crystal," Jana said.

"Take it," said Sylvia. "I don't want to have anything to do with it anymore."

Jana took the crystal from Sylvia. She then smashed it against a rock. A light grey mist exploded out from the crystal and flowed back into the dragon's body. The dragon stirred.

"Ceredos?" asked Jamie.

The dragon turned his head and looked at Jamie and Jana. He shook his head slowly and blinked a few times.

"You," said Ceredos. "You have spared me?"

"There's been enough death for one day," said Jana.

"I lost my soul," said Ceredos. "I felt doomed to spend eternity in a crystal prison. But you released me, Jana Aliston. I know that we dragons have not always been worthy of your trust, but believe me now. Your grace will not be forgotten."

"Forget it," said Jana. "I don't care anymore."

Ceredos rumbled to his feet. He limped around slowly, testing the strength of his leg.

"You have my sympathies for your loss," said Ceredos. "I wish there were something I could do."

"Could you?" said Jamie.

"No," said Ceredos. "That is beyond even our power."

"Go away," said Jana. "I want you dragons to go away. Leave us alone."

"As you wish, Jana Aliston," Ceredos said.

Ceredos stumbled aloft clumsily. He took to the air and flew off to the horizon.

"Come on," said Jana. "Let's go."

Anna Aliston's funeral was a quiet one. Westley and Mallory stayed to comfort Jana, and Jana's father arrived to visit as well. There were a few mages who came out of hiding to give their respects. It was otherwise a quiet and somber occasion.

Three days later, Jana and Jamie sat on a bench in the southern part of Westvalia's inner city. It was a sunny but cool day, and a fair breeze blew through the air. Jana was in a reflective mood.

"I can't believe she's gone," Jana said.

"I can't believe she is, either," said Jamie.

"My sister was never one for adventure," said Jana. "She came along with me a few times because I needed her help. She would have never gone off to get the flutterbees by herself. She only did that because she loved me."

Jamie nodded.

"It's my fault she died," said Jana. "She died trying to save me. I'll never forgive myself for that."

"It's not your fault," said Jamie.

"If it weren't for me," said Jana, "she would still be in Hockessin. She would be alive."

"You don't know that," said Jamie.

"Gods, I miss her," said Jana.

"I know," said Jamie. "I do too."

Jana cradled her head in her hands and looked down at the ground.

"You know, sprite," said Jana, "you proved yourself on that island. You showed me that you could handle being a mage yourself. You don't need me anymore."

"I want you," said Jamie.

"No," said Jana, "I think I'll give up this mage business. Everything we did, everything that we gained, it all means nothing now that my sister is gone. I think I'll just go see if Tybilt wants to marry me again."

"Don't say that," said Jamie.

"It's true," said Jana. "My heart isn't in it anymore. I don't want to be a mage. I just want my sister back."

"I know," said Jamie.

"The flutterbees will live," said Jana. "They will give you a bright future, where magic can help the kingdom soar to new heights. That future belongs to you, Jamie, not to me."

"You made it possible," said Jamie.

"I did," said Jana. "And yet somehow I wish I hadn't. That's why the future is yours to determine now."

Jamie nodded.

"It's over for me," said Jana. "I don't want to do this anymore."

15: THE END

James A. Whitney was and is many things, but most recently was a student of the Graphic Design Certificate Program in the Continuing Education division of the Rhode Island School of Design. Return of the Flutterbee is the fifth of a series of five books that was designed for the Final Studio class within the certificate program.

The design of this book would not have been possible without the help of the instructors and students within the program. The author wishes to thank Dina Vincent, Anya Lownie, Anne Marie Byrd, Bryan Rodrigues and Anther Kiley for their encouragement and instruction. He also wishes to thank Grace Bevilacqua, Jeffrey Bonderow, Amy Griffis, Pamela Gyles, Jamison King, Britton Koessler, Diana Lurio, Ainslee McAndrew, Rachel Sandler and Ann Wang for their friendship, invaluable critiques, and advice during the program.

The first draft of Return of the Flutterbee was written during National Novel Writing Month in November 2010. For more information on National Novel Writing Month, go to <http://www.nanowrimo.org>.

Finally, the author would like to thank his daughters Jamie, Samantha and Allison and his wife Sally for sticking with him through sickness and health, bad times and good.

Lightning Source UK Ltd.
Milton Keynes UK
UKHW022022070619
344049UK00013B/1108/P